Holmes Entangled

ALSO BY GORDON McALPINE

Woman with a Blue Pencil

Hammett Unwritten (as Owen Fitzstephen)

Holmes Entangled

A Novel

Gordon McAlpine

SEVENTH STREET BOOKS®
AN IMPRINT OF PROMETHEUS BOOKS
59 JOHN GLENN DRIVE • AMHERST, NY 14228
www.seventhstreetbooks.com

Published 2018 by Seventh Street Books®, an imprint of Prometheus Books

Cover design by Jacqueline Nasso Cooke
Cover design © Prometheus Books

This is a work of fiction. Characters, organizations, products, locales, and events portrayed in this novel are either products of the author's imagination or used fictitiously.

Inquiries should be addressed to
Seventh Street Books
59 John Glenn Drive
Amherst, New York 14228
VOICE: 716–691–0133
FAX: 716–691–0137
WWW.SEVENTHSTREETBOOKS.COM

22 21 20 19 18   5 4 3 2 1

Library of Congress Cataloging-in-Publication Data

Names: McAlpine, Gordon, author.
Title: Holmes entangled / Gordon McAlpine.
Description: Amherst, NY : Seventh Street Books, 2018.
Identifiers: LCCN 2017044811 (print) | LCCN 2017048882 (ebook) | ISBN
    9781633882089 (ebook) | ISBN 9781633882072 (softcover)
Subjects: LCSH: Holmes, Sherlock—Fiction. | Private investigators—England—
    Fiction. | Doyle, Arthur Conan, 1859-1930—Fiction. | GSAFD: Mystery
    fiction.
Classification: LCC PS3563.C274 (ebook) | LCC PS3563.C274 H65 2018 (print) |
    DDC 813/.54—dc23
LC record available at https://lccn.loc.gov/2017044811

Printed in the United States of America

To my Mother, for her many worlds

PROLOGUE

Buenos Aires, Argentina, 1943

Sr. J. L. Borges, 44, has completed his shift at the ill-organized Miguel Cané Municipal Library near the city center, where he works as first assistant. Now, as the final hour of daylight glows across the capital, he disembarks from the bus a few kilometers north of the library. With a battered briefcase in hand, he watches the bus pull away and then glances around to assure himself that no one else has disembarked and that no car or motorcycle has pulled suspiciously to the side of the road. He is no gumshoe, as in the American pulps, but he believes he'll know if he is being followed. For now, he feels all right. Besides, he suspects the next attempt on his life will come in the dead of night, as it did the first time.

He turns and starts up the street, which leads past his family's former apartment. He didn't plan this route with the old residence in mind. When he walks past, he doesn't glance at the window on the second floor, through which, as a younger man, he'd lean out in search of a breeze on blistering days. It is no absence of nostalgia that prevents his turning back; rather it is his myopia, which would produce little more than a blur from such a glance. Instead, he focuses on the sidewalk before him and continues toward the office of a private investigator in the nearby Palermo district. He's had no previous contact with the PI, nor has he come by the man's name and address through reputation, recommendation, or advertisement. Nonetheless, he knows who he is and where to find him.

This is because he dreamed of the PI a few weeks before.

No ordinary dream.

Naturally, Borges has many times experienced dreams that *seemed* real—dreams of a type that come to everyone. But this dream was different. This time, he knew with certainty upon awakening that the man in his dream was to be found in Buenos Aires exactly as he'd dreamed him. Back issues of the newspaper and a quick reference to the telephone directory confirmed it was so. Could this merely be a subconscious memory dredged up in sleep and disguised as an anomaly? No. Otherwise, how could Borges awaken knowing things about the PI that no one else knew—that no one else *could* know? Even more to the point, how could he know things about the PI that the detective did not even know about himself?

Initially, Borges took no action.

What was he to say to such a man, for whom graft and violence were of far greater interest than an obscure librarian's dream?

He might never have made contact, despite the strangeness.

But then, while alone and attempting to organize and catalogue the disarray in the library basement, he discovered among the stacks a handwritten manuscript in a small cardboard portfolio. Intrigued, particularly by the presumed author, he smuggled the manuscript out of the library and read it as soon as he got home. After finishing, he believed he understood how his strange dream of the PI might have occurred. In possession of such a manuscript and seized by the attendant information therein, as well as the attendant threat, he needed the PI's help.

Was it all of a piece?

Now, Borges takes a careful step over a blooming jacaranda tree's thick root, which has spread beneath the sidewalk, cracking and raising the cement by half a meter. He could have eased his journey to Palermo by transferring to a second bus or by riding the underground or, in such an important instance as this, by paying for a taxi to deliver him to the

PI's building; however, he chose instead to navigate the cracked sidewalks that lead from the Recoleta district to Palermo because he still has much to consider before arriving. Indeed, he even makes a detour through the vast Cementerio de la Recoleta, with its ornate, aboveground crypts, to plan how best to explain it all to the PI.

The manuscript is surely worth a king's ransom.

Since placing it in his worn briefcase, he has not allowed the attaché out of his sight (even while at work in the very basement from which he snatched the hidden treasure). Had he the proper hardware, he'd have handcuffed himself to the case, as they do in films and novels of espionage. When sleeping, he has slipped the manuscript under his pillow. What to do with such a thing? What to make of the manuscript's startling assertions?

Then, less than twenty-four hours ago, someone shot at him, barely missing.

He does not linger in the cemetery, as being there suddenly seems an unsettling omen.

Besides, the daylight is fading.

The PI's office is located on the third floor of a four-story building across the street from the Jardines de Palermo, an urban park where respectable gentlemen stroll with their women until darkness descends and the place transforms into a haven for trolling, beleaguered homosexuals and their nemeses, the *malevos*, hopped-up, knife-wielding young criminals (craven antitheses of the *cuchilleros*, the romanticized knife fighters of Argentina's storied past). The *malevos* prey on the poor sodomites, beating them, taking their money, sometimes stabbing them.

Since it is after working hours when Borges enters the office building, the elevator operators are gone. So he walks up the stairs. The building is designed in the arcade style, which allows for a vast space at the center, open all the way to an ornate glass ceiling. Art deco handrails line the walkways of the four floors. The frosted glass of office doors, bearing gold-leafed names and credentials of lawyers, accountants, and psychoanalysts are all dark, save one. This comes as no surprise to Borges; he knew the PI would still be in his office.

How did Borges know he would still be here? This too he dreamed. He opens the door and enters.

The anteroom is empty, but the door to the PI's private office opens before Borges takes three steps in.

The PI, mid-thirties, is tall and narrow. No bull of a man. But Borges suspects that beneath his wrinkled suit the man's body is hardened, like the smooth trunk beneath the soft, furrowed bark of an olive tree.

The men make introductions.

"So, Señor Borges, why have you come to see me?" the PI asks, inviting him into his office. He doesn't wait for Borges to respond. "I apologize that my secretary was not here to greet you properly with tea or maté. But seeing as she goes home at six . . ."

"It's better that we're alone," Borges interjects.

The PI looks at him. He grins. "Sounds serious. Maybe even dangerous. No problem. Serious affairs are my business." He moves around his large oak desk, which is littered with files, legal forms, cigarette rolling papers, a calabash gourd for maté, framed snapshots of race horses, a small chess board sans pieces, and pencils in many colors, which lay like random slashes of paint among the scattered objects. A telephone balances precariously at one edge of the desk and a green-shaded banker's lamp at another.

These items too Borges has dreamed.

The PI indicates that Borges should sit. "It's quite fortunate I'm available this evening. Usually, I operate by appointment only."

Borges removes his hat and sits in the wooden chair across the desk from the PI, setting the briefcase on the floor at his side but keeping a grip on the handle. "I knew you'd be here, available to me."

The PI looks confused. "How did you know that?"

"Because I dreamed you, sir."

The PI takes his own seat behind his desk. "Did you say 'dreamed'?"

"Yes."

The PI smiles. He slides open a drawer.

Borges wonders if he is removing a gun. But it is only a bottle of fernet and two water tumblers. The librarian smiles, reminding himself that not all PI's are like Humphrey Bogart in *The Maltese Falcon*, which he saw just a few weeks before at the *El Ateneo* movie house. Borges liked Sam Spade, who seemed made for his work—amoral, but still possessed of a personal set of values. Not all PIs are so well adapted. Some, like this one, are closeted intellectuals, less suited to the work than they believe.

"Drink?" the PI proposes.

Borges nods, though he prefers wine.

The PI pours, and they each down the strong, bitter spirit.

After allowing a moment for the drink to settle, the PI offers another.

Borges shakes his head, and the PI puts the bottle back in his desk drawer, leaving the two glasses as further detritus on the desk.

"So, you *dreamed* me, Señor Borges?" he asks, incredulously.

Borges takes a long, deep breath but remains silent.

This is not going to be easy to explain.

The PI swivels around in his desk chair to the back wall of the office, where a small bookshelf holds a confusion of books as ill organized as the desktop. He takes from the shelf a narrow volume and turns back toward Borges, holding up the book. "You wouldn't, by chance, be the author of this collection of essays?"

Borges can't make out the title. "My eyesight is quite poor."

"*A History of Eternity*," the PI reads aloud. "By Jorge Luis Borges."

Borges is surprised. The book was published almost eight years before and sold fewer than one hundred copies. In response to the indifference of the reading public, Borges swore off writing. To date, he has not broken his oath. Nor has he any intention ever to do so. He has resolved to be a librarian to the end of his days, as obscurity at least spares one from public humiliation. "How did you come by that?"

"I enjoy philosophically speculative works."

Yes, the character Borges dreamed *would* appreciate such things, even if few others do.

"So, are your claims that you 'dreamed' me one of your philosophical experiments, Señor Borges?" The PI tosses the book on the littered desk top.

"No."

"Research for a new book. A story?"

Borges shakes his head. "I gave up writing years ago."

"Then what is this all about?"

Borges looks around the office. With a wave of his hand, he indicates the framed pictures of clipper ships on the paneled walls. "This room is just as I dreamed it," he says. Next, he indicates the disheveled desk. "Also, just as I dreamed it." He looks directly at the PI. "And your impatient, scowling face is also the same as in my dream."

The PI sighs deeply. "Anyone could make such claims, Señor Borges. They prove nothing about your 'mystical' dream. Look, it's after hours. I am a busy man. Are you merely wasting my time?"

Borges leans forward, placing the palms of his hands on the only two open spots on the desktop. "Perhaps, then, I should share something of a more private nature regarding your life." He waits for the PI to respond, but there is nothing. So Borges continues. "You're working, quite secretly, on a murder case involving a renowned criminal," he states, flatly.

"Any confidence man could surmise that by my job and reputation."

"Specifically, you're investigating a series of murders that you believe follow a geometrical and Kabbalistic pattern involving the unspeakable four-letter name of God," Borges continues. "Quite esoteric."

The PI stands from his chair.

Borges remains seated. "I must warn you that if you follow through with your theory . . . well, it ends poorly for you."

"Is that a threat, Borges?"

The librarian shakes his head. "It is intended only as evidence that my dream of you was quite comprehensive, allowing me to know even what you've been thinking." He pauses. "As if I had invented you."

The PI says nothing.

"You still doubt me," Borges observes. "But isn't it true that you've shared your theory with no one?"

"No one is to be trusted," the PI snaps. "My enemy has spies everywhere."

"I am not among them."

The PI's eyes narrow even as he forces a smile. "There is a more common explanation for your knowledge of my private suspicions regarding the murder case, Señor Borges. Occam's razor suggests we favor it." He stops.

"Go on."

"It is this," he continues, gesturing buoyantly with his hands. "Suppose I am correct in my theory about this Kabbalistic pattern in the crime I'm investigating. And you, being a conspirator, are merely parroting back to me what you suspect I've come to know. Or, perhaps, you are testing my progress in the case."

Borges nods, acknowledging the possibility, inaccurate as it is. "Frankly, I am quite flattered you could consider me a master criminal. But it is not so. Your current case has nothing to do with why I'm here. So allow me a different, simpler sort of demonstration. Does it suffice to say that you now have three hundred and seventeen pesos in your billfold?"

"A parlor trick," the PI says dismissively.

"Please be good enough to count, sir."

Begrudgingly, the PI removes his billfold from his inside jacket pocket. He counts the bills.

"Well?" Borges presses.

The PI returns the billfold to his jacket. "A parlor trick," he repeats.

Borges says nothing, confident in the man's native curiosity, which he knows is even greater than his own.

The silence works.

"Fine, I will admit to being intrigued," the PI says at last. "But I still do not know what you want from me."

Borges reaches down to the side of his chair, flipping the lock on the weathered briefcase and removing the manuscript, which he sets in his lap. Next, with his forearm, he sweeps a quarter of the detritus from the desktop, heedlessly sending it crashing to the floor. On the open spot, he gently places the manuscript, which is a hundred or more pages long, handwritten in small, precise strokes. "I believe contained in this manuscript is the curious solution to the nature of my strange dream. And the manuscript addresses much else as well. Perhaps everything."

"You mean everything about the murder case?"

Borges shakes his head. "Nothing so trivial as that. When I say everything, I mean everything." To assuage the PI's discomfiture, Borges continues: "You see, I was, quite naturally, confused by my dream, which afterward seemed to have revealed an actual character . . ."

The PI interrupts, objecting. "You're calling me a 'character'?"

Borges waves away the question as insignificant. "But then I came upon this manuscript, misfiled among the stacks of the library where I work. I don't know how long it's been there. Perhaps all or most of the fifteen years since it was written. Nor do I know how it got there in the first place. But, believe me, it is an illuminating document."

The PI sits and looks at the sheets of paper.

"It is a heretofore unknown manuscript written in the hand of the world-famous British consulting detective Sherlock Holmes, the paragon of your profession," Borges declares.

"Holmes?"

"Written after Watson died. The late nineteen-twenties, which is also the period during which the narrative is set."

"The period during which Holmes himself died by his own hand."

"Yes, shortly after completing this work. The two events may not be unrelated."

The PI looks at Borges. "And the handwriting?"

"I compared the handwritten pages to published photographs of Holmes's letters. I can confirm that the handwriting matches."

The PI reaches for the manuscript. But he stops. "Well, congratulations on your discovery. Doubtless, it fulfills a librarian's ambitions. But, since you've already found such illumination, why do you need me? And what has any of it got to do with your 'dreaming'?"

Borges announces, almost casually, "Since I found the text someone has been following me, intending my death."

"Why do you believe such a thing?"

"Because last night he fired a shot at me. It was well after midnight. I'd had a dream, of the ordinary variety if there is any such thing, and I could not get back to sleep. I thought a short walk might serve as a constitutional. I got dressed. No one was out. But soon I spotted a man in shadow who seemed to be tailing me. He was very tall. Blond hair. Then the gunshot, which tore a chunk of plaster out of the wall beside which I was standing, a hair's breadth away."

"It could have been a common criminal."

"Then why did he depart after the shot? Why didn't he rob me?"

"Perhaps he meant only to scare you, Señor Borges. Perhaps you're already out of danger."

Borges shakes his head. "The tall man who keeps to the shadows has hovered about my house every night between midnight and four a.m. I need him to be identified. That is where you come in. Will you take the case?"

The PI looks away. "If this manuscript is what you say it is . . ." He touches the bundle of pages with his fingertips. "It would be worth a fortune to publishers and even more to those countless, obsessive true-crime collectors of mementos of the great Sherlock Holmes."

Borges nods agreement. "But this assassin wants more than just to acquire the manuscript."

The PI waits.

"He wants me dead."

"Why?"

"You will have to read the manuscript to understand."

The PI sits back in his swiveling chair as if he's had enough of Borges and his fantastical claims.

That's when Borges puts two thousand pesos on the desk. He has saved the money for a holiday to Europe. "Your reading fee."

The PI sits up straight once more. He nods and reaches for the manuscript. "I'll read it tonight at my home and get back to you tomorrow." He stands, as if to dismiss his new client.

Borges remains seated. "I can't allow the manuscript out of my sight, as its value is impossible to overestimate. And, in saying this, I refer to more than its monetary, collectible value, which you've already recognized. I'm paying you to read it now, while I remain here. Surely, you've worked harder in your career to earn a good day's wages." He indicates the stack of pesos on the desk. "A good month's wages."

The PI takes the money. He sits back in his chair. "So you'll just watch me read."

Borges nods.

The PI points across the room. "I keep a pot of coffee on the hot plate over there, Señor Borges. It may be a bit stale by now, being the end of the day, but I'm sure you know how to make a fresh pot. Everything you'll need is there." Then he reaches for the calabash gourd on his desk. "I'll have my maté, if you don't mind, as it promises to be a long night." He picks up the manuscript and reads the title aloud, "*Uncertainty*, by Sherlock Holmes—*a True Account.*"

He turns from the title page to page one.

CHAPTER ONE

ENGLAND, 1928

I am not who you think I am.

Nor am I who you think I *was*, which may be more to the point, considering the misinformation disseminated to readers of true crime by my late friend and chronicler Dr. John H. Watson. Oh, I acknowledge that his inaccuracies were never complete falsehoods but more matters of exaggeration, concision, or omission. Rather, it is I who bears responsibility for the single instance of pure fabrication in the accounts, namely, that I retired to a country life. Not so. Watson opposed the ruse. He argued it would be a breach of his "journalistic integrity," to which I reminded him of the paltry liberties he'd taken with details in his accounts of our cases. Unmoved, he demanded my reasons. I told him the truth: that I needed refuge from the reading public, who'd turned my London residence into a tourist attraction. So Watson set aside his "journalistic" ethics and, in a late account, described my having retired to a pastoral cottage with a lovely view, a housekeeper, achingly dull pastimes, and not the slightest hint of further, intellectual interest.

The ruse worked well, despite the explicit disclosures in early accounts of our cases that inactivity is the bane of my existence, suggesting that if ever I actually were relegated to the life of a country squire I would, before two full moons illuminated the insipid pastures, put no needle into my vein, as I did in my youth to ward off boredom, but a bullet into my brain.

So, if the great detective did not retire years ago to the country, doddering among harmless hobbies, then where has he been?

Patience, please.

Allow me to remain a moment longer in the confessional mode, hopeful of establishing that what is to follow is not akin to the single, aforementioned fictional enterprise I foisted upon Watson but is true down to its most minute detail. Thus, I must acknowledge one last misleading element of my friend's famous chronicles, which involves neither fabrication nor any of the minor dramatic license that characterized Watson's narrative strategies; rather, this chronic inaccuracy turns on subtler elements of style, tone, and attitude over which he had no real control.

Specifically, I refer to the Victorian sensibility of John H. Watson himself.

It is true that most of our recorded adventures occurred forty or more years ago during the Victorian era, gas-lit streets, and hansom cabs, so one may argue that there is nothing misleading about Watson's texts reflecting the values and tenor of the times. However, what complicates this justification is that among those values, particularly in cultured circles, was the propensity to paint over violence and mortality with either the absurd grotesqueries of the gothic or the banal consolations of the sentimental, both of which elevate bloody murders or premature death to perverse art. Inevitably, the solving of crimes was likewise elevated in the public consciousness from its gritty reality into a reassuring, ethical object lesson. In truth, the solution to a mystery usually proves a mere final, pathetic turn in a morally empty series of logically related events. Real crime almost never offers reassurance.

So, Watson was not insincere in his depictions.

He was simply a man of his time, a true believer in the inherent supremacy of Western (specifically, British) civilization. The death of Victoria did not spell the end of the era for my friend. Nor even did the slaughter of the Great War disillusion his view of nationalistic glory.

Indeed, on numerous occasions during the past decade, as my friend and I took the air together on the crowded promenades of London, he'd break midconversation to race across the street, dodging trolleys and auto-omnibuses, to hand five bob to one of the legion of crippled veterans (amputees, burn victims, the blind) who were scattered like wind-blown dandelions on street corners all over the capital. My friend's charitable impulse was all to the good. But in each instance he'd spoil his generosity by reciting Tennyson to the wounded wretches as he handed over the coins, "Half a league, half a league, half a league onward, all in the valley of Death rode the six hundred," determinedly unaware of the skeptical expression on the faces (or, in some cases, what passed for faces) of the disfigured boys subjected to his recitations. I'd usually have to pull Watson away or he'd recite the whole damn poem.

I loved him none the less for it.

Was *I* changed by the new century or the horrors of the Great War? Actually, no more than Watson.

But here's the difference between us: I never *was* a Victorian gentleman (and dash it all if I want to be remembered as one, however romantic the glow of gas streetlights or the clopping of horses' hooves on pavement may seem to the nostalgic legion who attend Leicester Square playhouses to watch actors in period costume portray me as a Victorian hero).

So, finally, the most significant inaccuracy in Watson's chronicles of our adventures was to suggest that he and I were, essentially, of like sensibility. His authorship was limited by his imagination, and he could not imagine my being anything but a Victorian gentleman. He often acknowledged in his writings my unconventional characteristics and habits, some of which were real, some misunderstandings. Once, when I told him I was both ignorant and indifferent as to whether the sun revolved around the earth or the earth around the sun, he took me literally and reported as much in *The Hound of the Baskervilles*. Absurd! Of course, many of my interests *were* esoteric. But, for all my eccentricities, Watson always held an unshakable confidence that I wanted to uphold the right, to deliver justice like an avenging angel, and to serve my monarch and country. As a gentleman, he could imagine me no other way. And I did uphold the right. But not out of commitment to right over wrong, whatever those words may mean to you or to anyone. And I did deliver justice, but only because others insisted on it and proceeded with its execution upon completion of my work. And I did serve monarch and country. But not *for* monarch and country. So what explains my years of single-minded work to solve complex criminal problems? Sympathy for the victims? What interest have I in the anonymous dead? Didn't the Galilean philosopher Himself say, "Let the dead bury the dead"? Alternatively, was it for money or glory that I practiced my relentless craft? Of course not. Such egotistic considerations are a waste of brain cells. The truth is I accomplished much as a consulting detective simply because it was my nature to do so, to hunt prey, as instinctual and absent of moral considerations as a lion stalking a gazelle. What more obvious phrase might I have employed with Watson to indicate such animalistic motives than "Watson, the game's afoot!"

But my friend never comprehended the atavistic nature implied in my enthusiastic imperative.

I was not who he thought I was.

Now, I am seventy-three years old. But I am no dinosaur, moving through the world unaware of my own extinction. I am a Modern, just as I've *always* been (even before there was such a term). Trust this: it is not I who has kept up with the age, but the age that has caught up with me. Yes I, the rational paragon, the human calculating machine designed to narrow all possibilities down to a single truth . . . but I have *always* known that some uncertainties never narrow to one truth. And this awareness might have been evident in Watson's chronicles except that he could never keep from adding his own modifying phrase to assuage his discomfort with uncertainty. For example, in "The Adventure of the Copper Beeches" he quotes me as follows: "I have devised seven separate explanations, each of which would cover the facts as far as we know them. But which of these is correct can only be determined by fresh information, which we shall no doubt find waiting for us."

No doubt find waiting for us?

I never said such a thing. I live in the real world. I always have. And there is always doubt as to what awaits us. My Boswell was incapable of accepting that I was literally suggesting there could be seven separate explanations, each as valid as any other, for perpetuity. For my chronicler, altering my dialogue (a mere phrase) was hardly a matter of choice. Doubtless, he recorded what he *recalled* hearing me say. He could recall it no other way. Why? Because Queen Victoria's Empire could not be built upon uncertainty.

But, like it or not, Modernity is.

Which brings us to these past years, placing me . . . where?

We've ruled out the country.

Still, you would never have found me—not if you were standing three feet away.

Nevertheless, I will tell you where I've been. I do so to set into motion this narrative, which, when finished, I will show to no one, but will arrange for its being transported and hidden unlabeled in the stacks of some disorganized library far away, to be found by a stranger perhaps decades from now, or, just as likely, never. You may ask: why opt for obfuscation when publication would please so many (my fame alone insuring publishing success)? After you read to the end you will need not ask.

☙

When it comes to my use of disguise, often noted in Watson's accounts, I have no secret method. Competence and attention to detail suffices. And so, under various assumed identities, I spent most of the past five years disguised as a variety of visiting lecturers at Oxford and Cambridge Universities—a new identity and area of expertise each term. For example, an exiled Russian expert in zoology, a disgraced Italian nobleman recognized as the world's leading authority on medieval alchemical studies, an American industrialist with controversial views on Economics that are reviled and respected by both capitalists *and* communists, and other such extravagant and expert personages. I attained these positions through counterfeited *curricula vitae* and actual publications in respected international journals in numerous disciplines, all under a repertoire of assumed names. This provided me with diversion as well as the occasional intellectual exchange with a brilliant young mind. And there was value even in my interactions with ordinary thinkers, including fellow faculty members, who, incidentally, were no more difficult to fool with my disguises than were the students. These ordinary exchanges kept me apprised of *the new*, be it Surrealism, Dadaism, jazz, the "hardboiled" school of American detective stories, German Expressionist cinema, and analytic philosophy (as an aside, I was the guest of Bertrand Russell for numerous "welcome" luncheons in the splendid dining hall of King's College, each time in one of my new guises, and even the famous sage himself has never been wise to my trick). This rogue academic life eased the passage of time. I was looking for nothing more, though I must say, not without a hint of pride, that there are few alive who could have accomplished such a ruse, particularly at such prestigious universities. By the time of this final case, I was, under a series of pseudonyms, a leading authority and contributor of major breakthroughs in half a dozen academic subjects. All without ever leaving England, even if the subject was Siberian tigers or Bauxite formations on the salt flats of Utah. Clues to significant academic advancements are always contained in the current literature, at least for one who is fully trained in the art of deduction. That is to say, me.

Nothing to brag about.

Indeed, my academic impersonations were always something of a bore, if truth be told. So why did I engage in such endeavors?

That is a question for which I hadn't a good answer, until recently.

❦

Everything changed earlier this year at St. John's College, Cambridge.

There, in my final guise, as a goateed, hunched, and slightly palsied visiting lecturer I'd named Heinrich von Schimmel, I conducted a weekly seminar, quite comfortable in the paneled, second-floor rooms I'd requested for their view of the college's finest Tudor period courtyard. This time, my expertise, or, rather, the heavily accented Dr. von Schimmel's expertise, was the history of classical physics, Aristotle through Newton. My recent publications on the subject had proven sufficiently important that the good Dr. von Schimmel had been offered a full lectureship at the Sorbonne (naturally, I turned it down, as I had no interest in lecturing on any subject for more than one term and, of equal importance, I wanted to remain close enough to London to occasionally enjoy the comfort of my townhouse, which, incidentally, is no longer located anywhere near the noisy tourist attraction that 221B Baker Street has become).

But Dr. von Schimmel would not finish the term.

It happened like this:

I had just completed the week's tutorial. While the last of my students clumsily gathered his writing materials to leave my rooms, I settled imperiously into one of the two comfortable club chairs angled at forty-five degrees on either side of a great, stone fireplace.

I lit a cigarette.

"Good day, sir," the ungainly student muttered, as he fumbled his way out, shutting the door behind him.

Alone, I closed my eyes and breathed deeply of the fine Turkish tobacco.

But after a moment, the door opened again. Had the young bungler forgotten something? Surely he hadn't returned to discuss the afternoon's lecture, as I'd given to Dr. von Schimmel an uninviting personality and a propensity to ridicule questions (perhaps I'd allowed the common British stereotype of German sternness to narrow my characterization, but no one gets his *dramatis personae* perfectly right all the time). I looked up with an aggrieved, Teutonic expression.

But it was no student standing in the doorway.

A man of nearly my years stepped inside, leaving the door open behind him. He wore a thick, walrus-style moustache and boasted the powerful body of a former cricket or rugby player who had taken somewhat too enthusiastically to second helpings of Yorkshire pudding. Still, the big man moved with a grace that echoed the athleticism of his youth. He looked familiar, though I did not at first place him.

"You must be looking for another room," I asserted in my thick German accent. "Please be on your way."

"Are you Professor von Schimmel?" His accent indicated that he'd been raised and educated in Edinburgh but had lived the past four or five decades in England, specifically Surrey and then London.

"Yes, I am Von Schimmel," I snapped. I took a drag on my cigarette, holding it in the continental fashion, between thumb and forefinger. "Who are you and what do you want?" I asked, exhaling the cloud of smoke.

He shook his head as if the words he sought would not come. He merely stared at me, fascinated or confused by my appearance. After a moment, he opted to answer only the first of my questions. "My name is Arthur Conan Doyle," he said, nervously rubbing his thumb and forefinger on the brim of the bowler hat he held at his side.

I should have placed his face immediately.

Conan Doyle was a writer of minor repute. He was best known for a recent novel featuring dinosaurs still existent in modern times, a series of Medieval-period romances, and an extensive history of the Boer War, for which he'd been knighted. I'd never read any of his books but knew about his oeuvre because his one foray into mystery fiction, a short story called "B.24," published decades before, had drawn the ire and, ultimately, the legal action of Dr. Watson, who believed it to be a barely concealed plagiarism of our true experiences involving Lady Bracken-stall. Watson and Conan Doyle settled their conflict and, to my knowledge, Conan Doyle never again ventured into detective writing. Still, I'd observed his name in periodicals. Some years ago he had written a few mercifully forgotten articles in support of two country girls who claimed to have photographed fairies; of late, most of his "nonfiction" work had consisted of essays expressing his ardent support of Spiritualism, the pseudoscience of séance room fraud.

Of course, I gave no indication of my recognition, as Von Schimmel would not know the name.

"Do you not ordinarily *knock* before entering private rooms?" I pressed.

He shook his head, embarrassed. "Please accept my apologies. I was outside in the hallway waiting for your tutorial to conclude. And when I saw that last student close the door behind him . . . Well, I should have knocked. My apologies. I wasn't thinking."

"This fine and ancient institution is unimpressed with 'not thinking,'" I said, drawing again on the cigarette. I crossed my legs, remaining seated even as he silently drew nearer, as if for a closer look. What was this middling scribbler up to? "Are you a student of physics?" I asked, disingenuously. "Perhaps you teach the subject at a provincial school? In any case, have you a question? I haven't all day for unscheduled consultations."

He looked confused. "No, I'm an author."

I shrugged, still in Teutonic character. "Then you're in the wrong department. The dabblers in literature are located in . . ."

"I haven't come here to talk to a professor," he interrupted, exhibiting the first sign of a laudable British backbone in response to my dismissive treatment.

"Then why are you here?"

"I'm here to speak to Sherlock Holmes," he answered.

At this, I stood up, surprised. "The famous detective?" I grinned, my costume dental apparatus prominent. Nonetheless, I may have betrayed a moment of dismay. But only a moment. "What makes you think an academic such as I could put you in touch with *Sherlock Holmes?*" I didn't wait for an answer. "How would *I* know him? Why would I want to? He is no intellectual, but, for all his overblown fame, is a mere, retired tradesman whose life's work was spent among the worst of Britain's criminal classes. Better for you to ask some pickpocket in Islington than a Cambridge don, don't you think?"

He hesitated.

"Oh, I forgot," I snapped. "You *don't* think."

For a moment, Conan Doyle looked perplexed. But he pressed forward despite what he failed to conceal as doubt. "It's not a matter of your knowing him, Professor von Schimmel. It's a matter of your being him."

At this, I sat down in the club chair again, as if staggered by the absurd assertion.

Actually, I was staggered by its accuracy.

How had he come to know what the best minds of England had for years failed to figure?

I thought of Moriarty, who was dead.

But who else was capable of unmasking *me*?

Nonetheless, as the unflappable Professor von Schimmel, I laughed at Conan Doyle. "Perhaps rather than directing you to the Department of Theoretical and Applied Linguistics, where aspiring novelists share fictions far less fantastical than the one you just proposed, I should offer you directions to Bedlam in London, which, despite being a ninety-minute train ride, may be where you can find the most help." I returned my attention to my cigarette. "Leave my rooms at once, Conan Doyle."

He didn't move. "You are Sherlock Holmes."

The certainty in his voice gave me pause. With the hand that held my cigarette, I pointed to the door. "Close it," I said, remaining in Teutonic character. "We wouldn't want any passersby to hear your absurdities. It would reflect poorly upon you, Conan Doyle. There are men of greatness and influence moving about these ancient halls. And, though I know nothing of you, I possess a sufficiently generous spirit to wish to spare you their censorious assessment."

He turned back toward the door.

Meanwhile, I considered.

My desk, which contained Watson's revolver, was at the far end of the room. Still, it wasn't so far. I could stand and move quickly, seating myself behind the desk in a manner consistent with an outraged academic, pistol near to hand. However, I hadn't any indication that Conan Doyle's intentions were sinister, however inexplicable his knowledge of my true identity. Additionally, his carriage and posture was inconsistent with that of an assassin. Indeed, the awkward introduction of his damaging knowledge suggested something more of a victim than a perpetrator.

I didn't get up to go to the desk but settled back in my chair.

He closed the door.

"Deadbolt it," I said.

He did as I asked.

I could have further denied his assertion, maintaining my persona and eventually seeing to his removal from my rooms by the porter or even the constabulary if necessary. My counterfeit *curriculum vitae* and other identifying materials were in perfect order. Knighthood or not, Conan Doyle was a mere scribbler, and he'd find no patience among the university administration for assertions about my identity that would strike them as deranged. However, there *are* times when my native curiosity outweighs practical considerations for the smooth course of my endeavors. Who had tipped him about my identity? Or, if he had come to the realization himself, how had he managed it? And why? I needed to know, so as he turned and started again toward me I indicated the club chair angled on the far side of the fireplace.

"Sit down and make yourself comfortable, Conan Doyle."

His eyes widened. "So you are Holmes," he muttered.

"I didn't say that. I said 'sit.'"

He did as I directed. "But why are you in disguise?" he asked.

At this, I decided to dispense with the German accent. "I'll be the one asking questions, my good man."

CHAPTER TWO

I miss John Watson for many reasons.

Most significant, of course, was that he was my friend and confidante.

However, at this moment, I miss him because his absence means *I* have to write this account of my final and most far-reaching case, however slow and thereby intellectually inefficient the process of writing may be. Perhaps I should have shown John more appreciation for the time he put into chronicling our adventures. It's not so easy to put pen to paper. The challenge, I find, comes less from ferreting out "the right word," as so many men and women of letters are apt to self-servingly complain, than from coping with the sheer boredom of it. I always told John that I would have allowed all of our cases to slip into obscurity before I'd have undertaken to personally write an account of any one of them. I told him *my* time was too valuable.

So what did John do in response to my arrogant implication?

He knew how to "get my goat."

I deserved it.

In the final collection of our case accounts, published just last year (almost two years after Watson's death), are two narratives told in the first person by me, absent the familiar persona of Watson as narrator. Of course, what is obvious even to the casual reader is that the voice in both stories differs little if at all from that in the other chronicles. It is, clearly, Watson's prose. I believe his effort to place the stories in my voice was his attempt to prove that after so many years of friendship he knew me well enough to emulate the manner in which I would relate such tales. In this, his failure was complete. But I hadn't the heart to say so when the pieces were first published in *The Strand*, as John's health was then rapidly declining and I had no desire to disillusion him. If he wanted to believe he knew me well enough to emulate my thought processes . . . well, at that stage, where was the harm? Once, of course, my pride would have demanded that I not only object but ridicule such overreach. But I had nothing left to prove. As must be obvious by now, my prose style bears little resemblance to his. Admittedly, he displayed a crowd-pleasing instinct for the melodramatic that I would be hard pressed to emulate even if I wished to do so. Nonetheless, I ask myself what advice Watson the chronicler would offer me just now in the composition of this narrative. I imagine myself speaking a sentence that in life I never spoke to my late friend: "What shall I do now, Watson?"

And I imagine his answer: "Get on with the story, my good man!"

So, it's back to my rooms in Cambridge.

❧

Conan Doyle settled his large body in the chair opposite mine, setting his bowler on an end table. He removed a cherry wood pipe from an exterior pocket of his tweed jacket and, displaying it like an auctioneer, silently inquired as to whether I objected to his lighting it. Crushing my cigarette into an ashtray, I indicated with a nod for him to go ahead. I watched him remove a pouch from an inside pocket and then pack and light the pipe. The scent of a strong, shag tobacco, as Watson preferred, wafted my way. I was impressed with the composure with which Conan Doyle completed the process, his hands steady. But then I recalled that he was a physician as well as an author. Ophthalmology, if memory served. Precise manual work. This explained the steady hands, even as his eyes betrayed uncertainty.

"So, you *are* Sherlock Holmes?" he inquired.

This time, for sport, I spoke again with Von Schimmel's accent. "Please explain yourself, Herr Conan Doyle."

He leaned back in his chair and sighed deeply, as if relieved. "So, it is you," he said, taking a fortifying puff on his pipe. "No authentic Cambridge don would tolerate so outrageous an intrusion and assertion as I have just made, sir. Surely not with an invitation to sit and smoke. Nor with a request that I 'explain myself.' After all, who asks such things of a madman, which I would have to be if you were indeed the German academic this institution believes you to be."

I was mildly impressed. Perhaps the mustachioed man was brighter than his somewhat pedestrian books or Spiritualist hobby would indicate. I answered without the German accent, giving it up for good with Conan Doyle. "You're wrong to assert that I am not an 'authentic' Cambridge don, if by that you mean an expert in his field who teaches it to Cambridge students."

"Your expertise is criminology."

"That is but one among many. If I may be allowed immodesty, my latest monograph on Newton's inspirations is groundbreaking in the field."

"But you're not Von Schimmel."

I removed another cigarette from my case. "What's in a name?"

"Everything, when the name is 'Sherlock Holmes.'"

"You flatter me, Conan Doyle." I lit the cigarette. "And, more importantly, you interest me, which is no mean feat. But my patience has its limits. Need I remind you that you've no way of proving we ever had this conversation?" I indicated the telephone on my desk. "With a call to the porter I could not only have you removed but likely charged with slander. So, as I requested once before, please explain yourself."

"You mean, why I am here and what I want from you?"

"Yes," I rumbled. "But I'd prefer you begin with how you determined who I was . . . that is, who I am."

Conan Doyle nodded. "It's all tied together."

"Isn't it always? Please, proceed."

He started in. "You may or may not know that I am the author of numerous novels as well as a distinguished, multivolume history of the Boer War." He paused. "The history was work for which I was knighted."

I gave no indication that I already knew this. Or that I was impressed, which I was not, having turned down knighthood myself on more than one occasion from more than one British monarch.

After a moment, he resumed. "Previous achievements and honors notwithstanding, my greatest source of pride these days are the numerous articles and lectures I deliver in support of Spiritualism, with which I am sure you're familiar, Mr. Holmes."

"I am familiar with the so-called 'field' of Spiritualism, but I cannot claim to be familiar with your articles or lectures."

Conan Doyle grunted and took a steadying puff on his pipe. "Let me get to the point. I was informed of your whereabouts and your clever, assumed identity at a séance conducted by the incomparably gifted medium Madam Du Lac, which I attended exactly five weeks ago."

At last, we were getting to what I believed was the problem. "So, who told you how to find me?" I asked.

"Stanley Baldwin."

"*The* Stanley Baldwin? Our current prime minister attended a séance?" I asked, incredulous. Perhaps a Labour party leader, but a Conservative? Never!

"You misunderstand, Mr. Holmes . . ."

I stopped him. "And please don't get into the habit of calling me by my real name," I requested. "It's rather a burden. A hindrance to investigation. And in the unlikely event we should be overheard by someone here at the university . . . well, it could cause some confusion."

"As you please," Conan Doyle acknowledged. Then a new thought occurred to him, its arrival as obvious in his changing facial expression as a train chugging into a station. "If I may ask, why *are* you disguised as a Cambridge lecturer?"

"You may ask, but I've no intention of answering."

"Then it's a secret project?"

"No, Conan Doyle. I choose not to answer your question simply because it serves me no purpose to do so. As I said before, *I'll* ask the questions."

Conan Doyle nodded, suitably chastised.

I continued: "Why would our prime minister stoop to attend a séance, which for a busy man engaged in real-world affairs must represent the most thorough waste of time imaginable."

Conan Doyle at once stiffened and seemed to expand, and for a moment I glimpsed him as he must have looked as a young man when he engaged as an amateur boxer and an oceangoing seaman (these biographical details were indicated to me by the ancient scar tissue about his knuckles and the seaman's inevitably life-long habit of using his free hand to shield his pipe from ocean gusts when lighting it, even indoors). Unselfconsciously, he further pumped up his body as his mind did the same. So I agitated him further.

"Séances are for desperate widows or for the kind of pathetically gullible men losing money to 'Find the Lady' card shams in Piccadilly," I continued. "Not for men who have real work, real purpose."

Rudeness too is an investigative technique.

In response, Conan Doyle's eyes narrowed just perceptibly, even as his rotund face reddened; now, I observed his expression set into a determined scowl, focused and concentrated, as it must have appeared decades before when he made a rugby tackle or approached the wicket as a cricket batsman. By so observing, I surmised that he was incapable of hiding his emotions. This made the likelihood of his being deceitful very small. Oh, he may have been a fool when it came to his ardent belief in Spiritualism, I thought at the time, but he was no liar.

"Of course, I don't mean to offend," I said, softening the moment.

He grunted. "No offense taken. Revolutionary new ways of understanding the world are always met with disbelief by men whose intellects..." He stopped, suddenly realizing the absurdity and ill advisedness of attacking my intellect as lacking either imagination, depth, perspective, or whatever other word with which he ordinarily concluded his oft-practiced defense of Spiritualism. "In any case, you misunderstand me, Mr. Holmes."

My real name again. I sighed at the beefy fellow's inability to follow the simplest directions. "You were speaking of Stanley Baldwin, our prime minister," I prompted.

"Yes, him. The prime minister and . . . um, *not* the prime minister."
He stopped, muddled.

"You're speaking gibberish, Conan Doyle, which I do not appreciate. And in this instance I am not merely referring to your support for Spiritualism."

"You may wish to temper your disapprobation of Spiritualism when you hear that the distinguished attendees at the séance, which was held at the lovely Mayfair home of Lady Vale Owen, included the Earl of . . ."

"Please spare me the distinguished company," I interrupted, well aware that an aristocratic bloodline did not insure common sense but rather increased the likelihood of its opposite. "You said the prime minister was among the party and that it was he who told you where to find me."

Conan Doyle shook his head. "You misunderstand, Mr. Holmes. I never said Stanley Baldwin was present among our party. Rather, he appeared to us as a spirit contact! It was in a spectral form that he communicated to me where I would find you and under what guise. He whispered it. No one else heard, so you needn't worry."

"Wait, the prime minister appeared to you as a spirit?" I asked.

"Yes."

"And others in the room saw this 'manifestation'?"

"Everyone. Naturally. But the spirit spoke only to me."

"Stanley Baldwin is *alive*," I said. "He made a speech before Parliament earlier today. Correct me if I'm misinformed, but aren't séances communions with the dead?"

Conan Doyle shrugged, sheepishly. "Obviously, it was no ordinary spirit manifestation."

"Obviously," I said, allowing the word to drip with misgiving. Ordinarily at such a juncture I'd have shown the middling scribbler the door, unwilling to waste further time. But the fact remained that Conan Doyle had discovered my identity when the best minds of England had failed for years to do so. It was important I discern how he did it. I didn't consider him deceitful. But that didn't make me a believer, either in Spiritualism or Conan Doyle's native reliability. "It seems you were taken in by a 'spirit imposter,'" I said, lightly.

"Your skepticism is wittily communicated, Mr. Holmes, and, frankly, in this instance, I do not hold it against you. I was skeptical myself." He leaned toward me, the bullish acrimony of a moment before dissipated. "Séances *are* communions with those who've passed on," he continued. "And yet, undeniably, Baldwin is alive. So what occurred that night at Lady Vale Owen's? Trust me, Mr. Holmes, the spirit that manifested was the real Stanley Baldwin and yet . . . not. Yes, he was born in Worcestershire. Yes, he was first cousin to Rudyard Kipling. Yes, he attended this very university and studied History at Trinity . . ."

I stopped him. "I don't need a biography of our prime minister. Every English schoolboy knows his background."

At this, Conan Doyle stood, unable to contain a turbulence within him. "But there's the rub, Mr. Holmes! The Stanley Baldwin who spoke to me during the séance *never became prime minister*. He'd been crippled by a runaway hansom cab at the age of twenty-nine. Do you understand? His spine was broken and, ever since, he's suffered from a pronounced asymmetry in his upper body and walked with a cane. So it's the same Baldwin, to a point . . . but then different."

I looked hard at Conan Doyle. What had I missed about him? By what gesture or inflexion or quivering eyelid/fingertip/neck vein might I perceive evidence that some wrinkle in his brain had become home to the malleable worm of deceit. Card sharps call what I was looking for a "tell." I am a master. But I still saw nothing. He seemed merely a naïf (more imaginative than most, blessed with above average intelligence, old-fashioned despite his "revolutionary" ideas about the afterlife, and, finally, well-intentioned). I couldn't help liking him, despite all. Why? The truth is he reminded me of Watson, though I feel I do my late friend injustice by the comparison.

"You remain skeptical, Mr. Holmes?"

My silence indicated my answer.

He began pacing the space between our chairs. "I too was skeptical," he repeated. "I am one of the world's leading experts on Spiritualism, and even I don't understand it. Can it be that from the 'other side' we contacted an alternative version of a man still living, *quite prominently*, among us? Ordinary spirits don't suffer from spinal injury symptoms. Death heals all that. But neither was he from this world. He was transparent, for God's sake. Just like other spirits I've seen."

I found almost entertaining the absurd notions of "ordinary" spirits or death as a healing mechanism.

"In short, I was astonished," he continued. "It's inexplicable! I can't claim to have been fully convinced until just now, when I walked into this room and discovered the famous Sherlock Holmes disguised as 'Professor von Schimmel,' just as I'd been advised by this 'other' Stanley Baldwin."

"The crippled one?" I interrupted.

Conan Doyle nodded. "It was all too bizarre, even for me," he mused. "And yet, here you are."

"Yes, here I am," I said, betraying neither skepticism nor encouragement.

Conan Doyle had offered no real answers, sincere as his attempts seemed. I still didn't know how I'd been found out. Or by whom. Or why? I knew séances were dens of criminality, victimizing the most vulnerable and heartbroken of England and beyond (being popular in America as well, despite the well-publicized exposés of charlatans by the famous magician Harry Houdini). Conan Doyle and other like-wise sincere supporters of Spiritualism readily acknowledged that fraud existed in many, if not most, séances. But they argued that fraud exists in banking and politics and personal relations, and yet we do not dismiss such endeavors out of hand merely because they are infected by a percentage of deceivers. Of course, this is a logically flawed argument. Nonetheless, Conan Doyle and his ilk are evangelical in their defense of the handful of "authentic" manifestations they consider to be proof of spirit contact. I didn't doubt his sincerity.

Interpreting my silence properly, Conan Doyle responded: "I am quite expert at ferreting out frauds," he said. "I have publicly exposed many. Do you not read the newspapers? Trust me, sir, I know all the tricks, some of which were demonstrated to me during my last trip to America by Harry Houdini himself."

"Yes, I'm sure you *want* to avoid being overly credulous," I acknowledged. "But . . ." I stopped, leaving the sentiment unspoken, but clear.

He straightened. "I am no fool, Mr. Holmes," he insisted.

I might have pointed out to him that in my long experience men who made that particular denial were almost always wrong in their assertion. But I said nothing so cruel. Likely, what stayed my biting comment was that the big man standing before me again reminded me of Watson, in his self-conscious manner and almost painful sincerity. Nonetheless, I remained clear: every day brought new, fraudulent techniques of fabricating what *appeared* to be semi-transparent figures, recognizable as dead personages, who seemed intent upon delivering messages to gullible, hand-holding Spiritualists. The technology of Spiritualist fraud surpassed even the work of most magicians playing our largest West End theaters. Despite Conan Doyle's claim of expertise, he was doubtless as easily taken in as any other believer. In short, a common dupe. Nonetheless, his presence in my rooms was uncommon indeed.

"So, how did this 'spectral' Baldwin know of my assumed identity and position here at Cambridge?" I asked. "And why would he share the information with you alone?"

"I don't know," he answered. "But the spirit recognized my face and approached, asking me in a whisper about your well-being, as if you and I were connected. Then he inquired as to how your secret identity as Professor von Schimmel here at Cambridge fit into the 'canon.' It made no sense to me. And that's all he said."

"You didn't ask for clarification?"

"It wasn't an interview, Mr. Holmes. It was a miracle."

A most unsatisfying answer. I settled back in my chair. Was Conan Doyle's far-fetched yarn intended to reveal a more mundane reality? Had I misjudged him? "Are you attempting to blackmail me, Conan Doyle?"

His nostrils flared just perceptibly, and his face reddened at my question. "Sir, your question offends me."

"Offense notwithstanding, I repeat it," I insisted.

"I am a man of honor," he snapped.

Judging from the further puffing-up of his chest and the broadening of his stance, I suspect if this were another era he'd have felt obliged to challenge me to a duel for having questioned his integrity. "I am here with no nefarious intent," he continued, "and would never dream of committing such a misdeed as you suggest."

I held up my hands to encourage him to calm himself.

He nodded and took a few deep breaths.

I waited.

After a moment, his face returned to a nearly normal shade.

"Since we are previously unacquainted, Mr. Holmes, I understand that you cannot know my character. Therefore, I excuse your inference. But you must trust that I am no blackmailer."

I believed him. "Glad to hear it," I said. I'd have had to destroy him if it had been otherwise. "So, why are you here?"

"Because you, Mr. Holmes, are here in Cambridge under the assumed identity of a German physicist, *just as the spectral visitor indicated.*"

Which begged the original question: who was behind the doubtlessly fraudulent "spirit manifestation" of our prime minister (supposedly crippled in some alternate world) and, more significantly, who had discerned my identity and whereabouts? Further, who had manipulated Conan Doyle to come to Cambridge and walk into my rooms, thereby serving to confirm my secret identity? Finally, how had this unknown mastermind discovered my secret in the first place, and why go to all the séance room trouble? It had the convoluted markings of Moriarty, but he was dead.

Did I consider that the séance of five weeks before might have occurred exactly as Conan Doyle had experienced it?

Ought I to have considered such possibilities? Well, that's easy to say now.

But who do you think I am?

True, I began this account by announcing that I am not who you think I am. But let's not get carried away.

I am Sherlock Holmes, and I am *not* given to considering metaphysics as a more likely explanation for anomalous experience than mere human frailty or greed. If you require an example, just consider my investigation of the legendary hell hound on the Baskerville estate. Hah!

So I likely would have dismissed Conan Doyle from my rooms, considering him the pawn of a more formidable opponent, useless to further investigation and perhaps even an impediment to whatever as yet unconsidered steps I would undertake to discover how my identity had been discerned and by whom. However, I did not dismiss Conan Doyle, as he chose that moment to remove his tweed suit jacket and begin disrobing before me. This took me by surprise.

"I do say, sir, what are you doing?" I inquired as he unbuttoned his waistcoat, removed it, and then slipped his braces from his shoulders.

He ignored my question, as if his disrobing was routine. "Ordinarily," he said, as he began unbuttoning his shirt, "I'd have come here five weeks ago to confirm the spirit manifestation's message. In my capacity as a psychic researcher, you understand. But . . ." He stopped.

I said nothing, still taken aback by his actions.

He continued unbuttoning the shirt. "I once had a minor legal entanglement over one of my short stories with your former associate, John Watson," he said. "So, wary of your being prejudiced against me, I was reluctant to call on you. I'm being quite frank, Mr. Holmes."

One button, then another and another . . .

"So, instead of calling on you immediately," he continued, "I focused on the manifestation himself, writing a paper for the *Journal of Psychic Research*, on whose board I sat. Oh, I was thrilled to share the shocking revelation that I had witnessed a spirit manifestation from an alternate version of a man *still alive* in our world, but quite different in some 'other' world. Remarkable! Amazing!"

"I find it amazing that you are disrobing, sir," I said.

He ignored my comment and continued. "Shortly after I submitted my article, wherein I made *no reference* to you or your whereabouts, my life was threatened in a series of telegrams." He slipped off his shirt, folding it carefully over the jacket on the backrest of a chair. All that remained now between his hefty, bare torso and the open air was a thin undershirt, which, with a painful grunt, he pulled over his head, revealing a bandage wrapped around his chest. A blood stain showed through, just below his heart. Being a physician, he skillfully removed the bandage and the pad of gauze beneath that covered the wound. "The threats proved real, sir. As you can see, I was shot."

I stood and approached him to examine the wound.

"You were lucky," I said, noting that his life had been spared by a sixteenth of an inch. This had been no staged attempt. "Did the surgeon manage to remove the bullet?"

"No, it's lodged too near my spine."

"Are you in pain?"

He shook his head. "Since the shooting, I've been taking a small dose of laudanum."

"So, who shot you?"

He shrugged. "I never saw a thing. Never heard the shot. I was walking alone through Regent's Park in the hour before sunset, trying to understand the implications of a spirit communication with a man existing in one state here but in a different condition in some other dimension, when I felt a sudden battering against my chest and all the wind went out of me. I can't even say it hurt. The next thing I remember was waking up in St Bart's, my family gathered about my bed."

"When was this?"

"About two weeks ago."

"And when did you get out of hospital?"

"This morning."

"So, the first thing you did was board a train and come up here to see me, alerted five weeks ago to my secret identity by . . . a spirit?"

"Sometimes, truth is indeed stranger than fiction, Mr. Holmes."

Watson too was fond of the cliché. I forbade him from ever using it in his accounts.

"You are, after all, Sherlock Holmes, and I need to know who wants me silenced."

"Do the authorities have any leads?"

"Scotland Yard? They're a rather . . . muddled bunch."

"Indeed." My assessment of Scotland Yard needn't be repeated here, as Watson made it clear in numerous chronicles. Suffice to say my opinion hasn't changed. "Do you have enemies?" I asked.

"Obviously, I have at least one," he replied, managing a grin. He placed the gauze once more over the wound and commenced rewrapping the bandage. "But I can't imagine who it might be. Oh, years ago I had a few brushes in court with men I believed were acting unfairly, prejudicially, or generally beneath the high standards of British gentlemen."

British gentlemen . . .

Yes, Conan Doyle was still as much a Victorian as Watson had been.

"But those legal cases were all settled amicably enough," he continued. "At least as far as I was concerned. Regardless, none of those men, whatever their failings, would ever attempt to *kill* me."

I thought he underestimated the propensity to murder. Nonetheless, I too suspected the attempt on his life had nothing to do with old court cases. "And the *Journal of Psychic Research*?" I asked.

"What about them?"

"Did they publish your paper?"

He shook his head. "The paper I submitted was the first of mine they ever rejected. I am, after all, their best-known author. And that's not all. I was removed from the board as well."

"They want to distance themselves from you."

"So it would seem." He pulled his undershirt back on.

I removed another cigarette from my case, lighting it as Conan Doyle dressed. I took a long draw. Then another, musing. When I turned back, he was rebuttoning his shirt. Somehow, he appeared less a bear of a man than he had when he walked into my rooms a half hour before.

"So what exactly do you want from me?" I asked.

"To get to the bottom of it, Mr. Holmes."

"You mean to find your assailant, see to his capture, and, in the process, insure your safety?"

He pulled the waistcoat around his broad midsection (it seemed a painful garment to wear for one with a gunshot wound beneath). "Well, find my assailant, insure my safety, and . . ." He stopped.

"And what?"

"Get to the bottom of it," he answered. "All of it."

I set the cigarette in an ashtray. "Surely you mean only the shooting. You can't mean 'getting to the bottom' of your mysterious visit from the ghost of our *still-living* prime minister."

"We don't like that term 'ghost,'" he said. "Besides, the manifestation was *not dead*. At least he didn't think so, and, generally, they know. The spirits I mean. Indeed, he seemed as disoriented by us as we were by him, whereas usually spirit manifestations are models of apprehension. If that makes any sense to you."

I shook my head.

"It doesn't quite make sense to me either," Conan Doyle admitted.

This was balderdash.

Yet here, in my rooms, stood Conan Doyle with a bullet lodged near his spine.

"I can pay you," he said.

"I don't need money."

"The spirit world would never have sent me to you if there was not something about this case that you *do* need, just as much as I need you."

"I don't believe in your spirit world."

"Still, there's something about this case that you need," he repeated.

"Such as?"

"I wouldn't know, but perhaps you do," he answered.

Since the onset of Watson's final illness and subsequent death I'd taken no cases, preferring to disappear into a mythical country retirement and an actual academic anonymity.

"What will it be, Mr. Holmes?" he pressed.

I said nothing.

"Or do you really prefer I call you Professor von Schimmel?" he added, pointedly.

Suddenly I felt ill at ease disguised as an old German.

Dash it all if the scribbler standing before me wasn't cleverer than I'd accounted.

CHAPTER THREE

Observing the accumulated pile of papers now on my writing desk, which I've labeled chapters one and two, I can't help but consider what Watson would make of my account to this point. Surely, he'd have progressed farther into the plot by now. Publishing most of his case accounts in *The Strand Magazine*, he knew his readers preferred a story that could be consumed from beginning to end on a twenty-minute omnibus ride. Understanding the public's appetite for adventure and violence, he'd likely have arrived by now at least as far into this narrative as the incident of my moonlit confrontation with an armed assailant in Kensington. In my telling, this incident likely will not occur for at least another chapter or two. But Watson knew his audience and why he was writing (first for money, and second for posterity). Do I know for whom I am writing and why? No. But I suspect, at this point in the endeavor, I may be writing in order to discern the answers to those questions. For whom and why. The truth is I may be writing for no one.

Perhaps that is disingenuous.

Perhaps I know exactly who I'm writing for and why.

Either way, I will move forward now at a gallop, akin to Watson, for at least one page, by summarizing how my meeting with Conan Doyle in Cambridge concluded.

After agreeing to take the case, I told Conan Doyle that his wife must relocate abroad until I settled matters to our satisfaction and, in the meanwhile, that he must take refuge himself in a safe house I keep in Bloomsbury. At first, Conan Doyle objected, citing his reluctance to be apart from his wife and his unwillingness to cancel his busy schedule of public appearances in support of Spiritualism. I pointed out that the grave would inflict a far longer separation from both his wife and his speaking engagements. He eventually allowed me to book immediate passage to the Continent for his wife and to get him safely started for my safe house in Bloomsbury. Thereafter I wrote a letter of resignation, signed by the venerable but apparently unreliable Von Schimmel, claiming he had experienced a family crisis that necessitated his immediate leave. I placed the letter on my desk to be found in the morning. Next, I telephoned long unused contacts throughout Britain, setting them to ascertain if our distinguished prime minister might possess a cousin or even an illegitimate brother of appropriate age who could have impersonated Baldwin in the vexing séance (a line of inquiry that ultimately revealed no leads). Finally, I crossed the deserted university grounds to the darkened Cavendish Laboratory. There, I slipped a note under the office door of my colleague Paul Dirac, a twenty-six-year-old physicist of startling brilliance who was engaged in the nascent field of quantum mechanics. As Dr. von Schimmel, the Newtonian, I had enjoyed Dirac's stimulating and enlightening company over meals in the dining hall. In my parting note, I encouraged the young man to keep me apprised of any new papers or associated developments in his research, including as my contact address a second safe house that I kept in the crime-ridden, dilapidated Islington neighborhood of London. Thus, by midnight, I'd freed myself of academic obligations, set the mechanism of investigation into motion, and took sociable leave of a brilliant acquaintance.

That night I passed into sleep in my own flat in London.

Now, be honest. Could Watson himself have moved the story along faster than that?

Well, perhaps he could. But there was ever only one Dr. John H. Watson.

❧

The following afternoon, I put my London flat in order, checked on Conan Doyle's comfort at my safe house, and enjoyed lunch at

Simpsons in the Strand, where I not only formulated an initial plan for my investigation but also played chess with Henry Atkins, the recent British champion (it would be immodest and ungentlemanly to reveal who won). Next, I screwed my courage to the sticking point and made my way to the comfortable, Belgrave Square townhouse of Dr. Watson's widow, on whom I had not called since the day of my friend's funeral. Three long years. The source of my trepidation was not merely shame at my neglect of the good woman; it was also that I had spoken to very few personal acquaintances as myself, Sherlock Holmes (being more often concealed in one or another of my academic personae), since I'd last visited the Watson townhouse. I know that stopping to make a social call at the inception of an investigation may seem an inexcusable dalliance. After all, I could assign to it no urgent analytical value. But three years is a long time for a man to be largely absent from the world, even longer for him to be absent from himself. And, frankly, that had been my circumstance. I am not the stock Holmes who struts and frets the boards of London theaters, flawless. So, before I embarked on the new investigation, I wanted to confirm that I could still be the Sherlock Holmes I had once been. The consulting detective. And the best way to do that was to return to the place where I had lost him.

John's widow and I had been acquainted for decades.

She may be familiar to you by her previous name, Mrs. Hudson, our long-suffering landlady at the Baker Street flat. This may take you aback, since, in films and theatricals, she is often mistakenly portrayed as being far older than Watson and me; John himself laid the ground for this misconception by offering no physical descriptions of her in any of his accounts, a literary oversight likely intended to assuage the chronic, unreasonable jealousy of his first wife, Mary. The truth is that Mrs. Hudson was quite young when she lost her first husband in the Anglo-Zulu War, and was still in her late twenties when I took rooms in her house. Nonetheless, in the years Watson and I lived there together, I never perceived an attraction between the two. Surely, I'd have noticed. Or perhaps not. Romance is, after all, one area of human experience for which I possess less than extraordinary acumen. In any case, John suffered ill luck in his first two marriages, both of which ended in divorce, before finally commencing a late-in-life courtship with Mrs. Hudson. Now, it was almost six years since they had married. On that nuptial day, each was a septuagenarian; she looked lovely with flowers in her grey hair, and he looked dashing in his old regimental uniform, even if it had been let out more than once since he'd first worn it almost a half century before. I believed their union promised a reasonable degree of happiness. The two spoke enthusiastically of exotic travel to Asian lands and sunny, carefree French Riviera retreats, which royalties from John's writings placed well within their means. However, in the first year of the marriage, he was diagnosed with a virulent cancer.

They never made it abroad.

While still a newlywed, Mrs. Watson proved her mettle by the selfless care she administered to her husband through his fatal illness. Of course, I already knew she was a patient woman. I had tested that patience myself by exposing her to the eccentricity, irregularity, and general atmosphere of violence and danger that hovered about my years at 221B Baker Street. Still, none of the forbearance that my lifestyle demanded of her as a landlady compared with the challenges of John's final, two-year-long illness.

Dying is a hard business.

Having seen so much of it in my work, I thought I knew.

But the experience of John's death proved an education for me.

Enough said about that for now.

I had bought a colorful bouquet of snapdragons at Covent Garden, which I enthusiastically extended when the door of the Watsons' townhouse opened before me. But it was not Mrs. Watson who opened it; rather, it was her housemaid. I should have expected as much, but the Watsons' wealth still came as something of a surprise. Of course, I'd been pleased for John. Just as I was pleased that the former Mrs. Hudson, who'd worked so hard and for so long, could now employ such help. Being somewhat uncomfortable with social calls, I awkwardly withdrew the bouquet from the poor housemaid even as she reached for it, as if I did not want her to touch it.

"For Mrs. Watson, I presume?" she said.

Was she referring to the flowers or to my visit? "Yes, the flowers are for Mrs. Watson," I said.

"I can take them and put them in water," she answered, her composure exemplary. "She'll be so pleased."

I handed them over. "And I too would like to call upon her," I said, perhaps unnecessarily.

"Of course," she answered, smiling. "Have you a calling card I may present?"

When I said nothing, she looked at me more closely.

Her smile disappeared and her eyes widened. She'd recognized me.

I'd left my flat that morning with only a felt fedora pulled low over my face as a disguise. I have found these past years that I usually can pass through crowds without being recognized merely by *not* wearing a deerstalker cap, which has become so widely, if inaccurately, associated with me that I am now thankful for the freedom of movement its absence allows when I go out sans disguise. However, my face remains well enough known, from the pen-and-ink portraits that accompanied newspaper articles about the crimes I solved, that when I am viewed up close I am still recognized (or, quite perversely, mistaken for William Gillette, the American actor and playwright who has made his career portraying me on the stage and in the cinema).

"You're Sherlock Holmes!" the young housemaid said, barely containing her excitement.

I nodded and bowed to her, attempting to compensate for the ill-mannered fashion with which I'd yanked the flowers away from her. "I am at your service, Miss."

She ushered me into the entry and closed the door behind us. Taking my cloak and fedora, along with the flowers, she disappeared through the small library, muttering, "I'll let the Missus know that you're here, Mr. Holmes."

"Thank you," I called after her.

A moment later, Mrs. Hudson emerged, her arms open wide. "Sherlock!"

I did my best with her affectionate hug.

"Come, come!" she urged, leading me into the sitting room. Once there, she turned and looked at me. "It's good to see you, Sherlock."

"And you, Mrs. Hudson . . ." I answered, catching myself just after the inaccuracy slipped from my lips. "That is, Mrs. Watson," I corrected.

Some habits die hard.

"I'm only a few years your senior, Sherlock," she said. "You're no longer my tenant. I married your best friend. So when *will* you call me by my first name?"

This is the sort of talk I find difficult (except when I am disguised and in character). So I said nothing.

"Please sit," she said. "Some tea?"

"That would be pleasant."

She rang a small bell, summoning the housemaid, and requested the refreshment.

"You look quite well," I said to her after the housemaid departed the room. "A bit older, but still hardy."

She did not respond to my apparently fumbled attempt at a compliment. "Sherlock, where have you been all this time?"

"The funeral . . ." I muttered.

She leaned toward me. "John's funeral? What about it?"

The funeral had caught me unawares. I am not one for religious mumbo-jumbo, ceremonial platitudes, or any of the myriad sentimental customs associated with the disposal of the dead. Nonetheless, when it came my turn to drop a handful of dirt into the murky hole and onto John's casket I found myself . . . well, not myself. So I endured the post-funeral social function at the Watsons' townhouse by assuming an identity akin to Sherlock Holmes but not Sherlock Holmes, like the actors who portray me in provincial theatricals. Why? Because if I remained myself I'd have run the risk of revealing too much. The other mourners seemed not to notice the difference. Mrs. Watson, understandably, was distracted by her own grief. I left as soon as it was socially plausible, resolved not to return until I might do so as the true Sherlock Holmes. Who knew it would take so long or how many times I thought it would *never* happen? But I explained none of this to Mrs. Watson, afraid that it could too easily be misconstrued as an *excuse*. One thing is certain; I seek no excuses for my life.

"I'm sorry to have been out of touch," I said to her.

"There's no need to apologize Sherlock," she answered. "I've just been worried about you."

"Worried? Why?"

"I knew that business about your retiring to Sussex was a ruse you'd cooked up with John."

"Yes."

"So you just seemed to have disappeared."

Indeed, that's how it would have seemed.

"So where *have* you been?" she asked again.

"Cambridge and Oxford," I answered.

"Working on cases?"

I shook my head. "Lecturing at university. In numerous fields."

She was unable to conceal her surprise. Likely, she struggled to reconcile my answer with my well-known lack of patience for underlings (including students of merely above average intelligence) and my general intolerance for the domesticity often associated with academic life.

"How is it that Sherlock Holmes has been lecturing in England and I never read news of it in the papers?" she asked.

"I lectured under assumed identities."

"Oh. Yes, you were always good at disguise."

"A necessary requirement of a consulting detective."

"But you weren't working as a detective." She held her teacup to her lips without drinking. "You were disguised to protect your privacy?"

"Of course," I answered. "And . . ." I stopped.

"And?" She said nothing more but held my gaze with unblinking eyes.

"I suppose I'd grown tired of being Sherlock Holmes," I said, surprising myself with my candor.

"Tired? But you *are* Holmes."

I nodded in acknowledgement. "Surely one can grow tired of one's self."

"And when did this particular weariness descend upon you?"

I answered without thinking. "About three years ago."

"Oh."

I'd said more than I'd intended.

About then the housemaid knocked, opened the door, crossed the room, and set the tea before us.

"Thank you, Charlotte. I'll pour," Mrs. Watson said. "That'll be all."

The housemaid departed.

Alone again, we were silent for a moment as she prepared our tea.

"Just as you like it," she said, handing over my cup and saucer.

"Thank you, Mrs. Watson."

"John passed on three years ago," she observed.

"Yes, but he put up a good fight."

"He would. That was his nature. But it's not my point."

I put down the tea cup. "Please, I came to visit *you*, my dear Mrs. Watson, not Dr. Freud."

She ignored my dismissal. "It's not so remarkable that John's dying would have an effect on you."

I'd lost control of the encounter. "Forgive my self-indulgence, Mrs. Watson. I didn't come here to talk about myself. I came to inquire how *you've* been."

She ignored my assertion. "Maybe it's that for all those years and through all those 'adventures,' John was your witness," she said. "And absent him . . ."

I waited, but she said nothing more.

Her habit of leaving sentences unfinished to serve as questions proved quite disconcerting. I gave her an unfinished sentence of my own. "I hadn't thought of it that way, but . . ."

She put her hand on mine. She smiled. "But now you've taken a case," she said, knowingly. "Mr. Sherlock Holmes."

"Yes."

"Can you tell me about it?" she asked.

"First, tell me how you're doing."

"You mean without John?"

"In general," I asserted.

"That means 'without John,'" she rejoined.

"Yes, I understand."

After Mrs. Watson's account of her adjustments to John's absence, which, in consideration of her privacy, I will not detail here, I acceded to her request and told her about the new case. One question led to another and, finally, just before her housemaid returned to remove the tea and accoutrements, I suggested, quite on a whim, that Mrs. Watson join me in the investigation, specifically the next evening at a séance. We could disguise ourselves as a married couple still bereaved by the loss of our only grandson a decade before in the Great War.

"A séance? How exciting," she answered. "It's quite an honor to be included in your investigation, Sherlock."

"This morning, I contacted Madam Du Lac, the medium whose encounter with the alternate, crippled version of our prime minister initiated the events that put a bullet into Conan Doyle," I said. "Under an alias, I secured all eight seats at her mystic table; while she does not ordinarily operate on such short notice, my offer of three hundred pounds sterling doubtless served to move the spirit."

"Moved the spirit. Very good, Sherlock," she said.

I shrugged, having intended no such pun. "Posing as a couple will make my infiltrating the séance room easier," I said.

"May I play the part with a Cockney accent?" she asked. "I can do one quite well."

I shook my head. "You'll want to change yourself as little as possible, in order to remain credible."

"But you'll have to disguise yourself, Sherlock," she observed. "After all, you're famous."

"Yes." We still needed to fill in the details of our assault upon Madam Du Lac, and to make contingency plans in the event of the unexpected. "Shall we get down to business then?"

"Can you stay this evening for dinner?" she asked.

Rather a non sequitur, I thought. "Well," I said, hesitating. I had planned on attending a West End Magic Show to observe the latest in legerdemain (in preparation for whatever tricks the spiritualist might have up her sleeve). But, sitting in the Watsons' comfortable parlor, I realized I likely already knew all the tricks. "Dinner's actually quite a good idea," I answered. "It will help us to develop the appearance of marital affinity, Watson."

Our subsequent preparations for the séance proved satisfactory.

The only awkward moment occurred during the dessert course, long after I'd laid out the case's precipitating events and a few of my, as yet, untested theories, when Mrs. Watson asked, "Do you think there is any chance we might contact our dear John on the other side?"

Had she heard nothing of my view of Spiritualism, expressed rather strongly during the main course?

Or had she heard but disregarded it?

Or is blind hope an irresistible force?

In any case, I answered empathetically. Perhaps not as gently as some; gentleness is not a well-developed facility of my communication skills. Nonetheless, I acknowledged how much she missed John. I missed him too. Maybe I missed him as much as she did, if in a different way. Or, perhaps, not so different. In any case, I assured her that Spiritualism was a confidence game that preyed on the vulnerability of the bereaved. I explained to her how mediums often used clandestine research to produce what seemed authentically personal manifestations or messages. Of course, as we'd be attending Madam Du Lac's next séance under assumed identities, any manifestation created for us would be as fictitious as our *noms de guerre*.

"So we won't even see a counterfeit spirit of our John?" she asked.

I shook my head, but said nothing more.

Our John.

❧

The next morning, I made my way alone to the London offices of the Society for Psychic Research, which had rejected Conan Doyle's recent journal submission and then had promptly cast him from its board, just days before he was shot. The society's offices were located in a house rather than a commercial building. Like its neighbors, the house was painted as white as the paper upon which I am scribbling these words. Eldon Road in Kensington, just south of Hyde Park, a distinguished neighborhood for such offices.

I arrived in the guise of an East Indian medium. (Earlier that morning, I had applied skin cream and blended compounds of my own invention to my face and hands, ordinary theatrical make-up being ineffective for close-up, personal interactions; I attached with spirit gum a false grey beard as tangled as a timberland thicket and attired myself in a turban, an extravagantly embroidered *sherwani* coat, which indicated both wealth and caste, and, for final effect, a colorful *dupatta* scarf, suggestive of the flamboyant character of my carefully crafted, new identity.)

"I am Siddhartha Singh," I said to an attractive young woman sitting at the reception desk of the stately journal office. The name too I had chosen for its flamboyant euphony and self-evident falseness, as mediums created their personas as broadly as politicians or cinema stars. My undertaking required that I appear as anything but an ordinary immigrant. "I am here to see Sir Charles." My Rajasthani accent was, if I may be allowed to place truth above humility, *perfect*.

Sir Charles Pendleton was president of the society.

"Have you an appointment?" the young woman asked. Her accent revealed her to be unexpectedly well-bred, likely the daughter or niece of a viscount, or perhaps an earl; in either case, her background was of higher standing even than that of her employer, Sir Charles. Thus, she was here for one of three reasons: first, out of a true passion for Spiritualism (allowing her to undertake a situation so far beneath her breeding); second, as a result of the increasing incidence of noble families coming upon financial ruin (some even losing their estates); or, third, and most intriguingly, as an operative (of what or whom?) in the guise of a mere office girl.

"I have no appointment Miss," I said. "But it would be much to Sir Charles's advantage if he saw me immediately."

She glanced me up and down. "He has no opening in his schedule," she answered dismissively. She feigned returning her attention to an ordinary invoice on her desk. "Perhaps if you called on us again next month we could get you an appointment." She trailed off, finished with me.

I looked around. As the building had not been designed as an office but a house, her desk was located in what would ordinarily have been the foyer, which featured fine Carrara marble and an exquisite chandelier. A tight, circular staircase rose up to the first floor. At either side of the foyer were sets of double doors, closed. The society appeared to be more than merely solvent.

I pointed to the invoice before her. "Castor and Sons," I said, reading the letterhead. The figures on the page beneath were of no consequence. "Well-known custom cabinet makers," I continued. "That does not seem like an invoice you'd want the general public to see on your desk, Miss. After all, we mediums are often accused of fraudulently using specially manufactured, 'trick' cabinets in our séances."

She looked at the invoice.

"This is for bookshelves recently built in Sir Charles's office," she snapped, turning her gaze up at me with disdain. "Entirely legitimate. Only a fraud himself would imagine that the public would be so suspicious of a mere invoice."

I lowered my eyes as if chastised. Nonetheless *my* suspicions had been confirmed. Castor and Sons was no cabinet maker, but a supplier of office goods, familiar to every real office worker in the city. She was as much a fraud as Siddhartha Singh.

But I still didn't know what game we were playing.

"I am a medium of great importance," I said.

"I haven't heard of you, Mr. Singh," she answered, her cultured voice expressing an impatience that seemed almost unbearable to her. "And I *am* familiar with all the important mediums in this city."

I thought this true, as she'd likely studied the membership roles of the society.

"As I said before," she continued, literally *shooing* me away with one hand, "Please come back next month and maybe then . . ."

I interrupted: "Doubtless, you *would* have heard of me if your organization was not so Anglocentric. Mysticism has been an integral part of my culture for untold centuries." I was unwilling as yet to leave the premises. After all, I hadn't delivered my intended message.

"That's an impertinent charge," she snapped, quite convincing in her role as offended acolyte. "Some members of our society and many contributors to our journal are not English. Some are even East Indian, such as yourself."

I bowed in apology. "I meant no offense, Miss."

"Oh? What else could you possibly have meant, Mr. Singh?"

"I meant only that your organization's work to date has been admirable, but incomplete. I am here today to help you complete it. To paraphrase your great bard, 'there are more things in Heaven and Earth than are dreamt of in your philosophy.'"

She huffed. "That quote could be the very motto of this organization, my good man."

"Yet the thesis of your work is that psychic mediums communicate with the dead."

"Of course."

"True, but that is only part of it," I said. "Very recently, for example, I conducted a séance in which, quite unexpectedly, my contact on the 'other side' was an astral body of a man whose *physical* body is still quite alive, here in London! The same man, yet not the same. You see, my spirit contact had become a desperate drug user, his life one of squalor, whereas his still-living counterpart had avoided the addiction and was a successful businessman. How to explain such a thing! Naturally, I am committed to publicizing this strange phenomenon. But first I want to discuss it all with Sir Charles. As soon as possible, Miss."

By now, her expression had changed, her disinterest replaced by the tightest concentration. Likely, such a report was what she had been sitting here awaiting. "Your strange psychic experience is indeed of the utmost importance, Mr. Singh. So I *will* arrange for you to speak with Sir Charles, who arrives back in London this very evening from a voyage abroad." She paused, considering the situation. "As he can't be here much before midnight, may I ask you to return here tonight at that hour to meet with him? Unusual, indeed. But for a matter of such importance, I know he would not want to let even one evening pass without consultation. Will that do?"

"I can come back tomorrow during normal operating hours," I offered.

"Oh no. I think for a matter of this importance Sir Charles would want to meet with you as soon as humanly possible."

The séance was scheduled for nine o'clock. The timing would just work. I nodded. "Midnight will do."

Yes, midnight would do to give them sufficient time to set an ambush.

But sometimes a mouse must tap at a trap to find the exact spot at which it will spring. A mouse of extraordinary acumen, that is. The danger is only in being caught unawares, a habit I have assiduously avoided lo these many years.

"Thank you, Miss," I said, exiting.

And just who did I believe was preparing such a trap? Not the Society for Psychic Research. While I did not share their tenets about an afterlife or the ability of mediums to make contact with its spectral inhabitants, I found highly unlikely the possibility of such a group of ardent believers wishing to quash *any* new aspect of their controversial "science," which thrived precisely on the continual development and publicizing of novel theories and marvels. Even less probable was their resorting to violence (Conan Doyle's gunshot wound, for example). Instead, the fraudulence of the receptionist suggested that the authentic leadership of the society, including Sir Charles himself, had been "removed" from the scene, to be found neither at midnight nor anytime soon. To confirm this, I spent the remainder of the afternoon and much of the evening, still in the guise of Siddhartha Singh, seeking the other officers and board members of the society, ultimately confirming that each was away from England for unspecified periods, traveling on diverse matters either personal or business related. The decades-old society had effectively been disbanded, at least temporarily, without the general membership or even the families of the absent leaders noticing.

I marveled at the feat.

Remember, the society was not without powerful members. Conan Doyle himself did not lack for influence, and he was but a small fish in the larger pond of notable or aristocratic members of the society. So what organization or individual was capable of compelling the movements of powerful men as if they were mere chess pieces, ultimately removing them completely from the board without anyone even taking note?

Once again my old nemesis, Moriarty, the Napoleon of crime, came to mind.

But wait.

Perhaps with that last comment, I inadvertently may be inserting into this true account a "red herring" of the sort indulged by Miss Christie and other contemporary mystery novelists of her ilk, which is not my intention. To avoid such claptrap, allow me to confirm here and now that Professor James Moriarty indeed died many years before these events. No Oriental wrestling trick saved *him* from the churning waters of the Reichenbach Falls. Be assured then that he plays no part in this mystery, however many times I suspected his evil genius during the investigation. Of course, Watson would likely scold me for breaking the chronological sequence of my narration in the manner of this paragraph. ("How could you be sure at such an early stage of your investigation that Moriarty had *not* somehow faked his death, just as you once faked yours?" he'd press, if he were looking over my shoulder now as I write. "Remember, Holmes, you should reveal in the course of your first person narrative only what you knew at the time," he'd insist, "as that is how professional writers sustain suspense! So why rule out the intriguing possibility that Moriarty *might have been* alive and behind the plot, even if he weren't?")

Ah, but I am a consulting detective, not a professional writer, however many scholarly monographs I have published under assumed names.

And I find "red herring" most distasteful.

Still, I acknowledge your good suggestion, Watson.

So I will make no habit of nonsequential intrusions in my narrative, though neither will I swear off them entirely. Does that satisfy you, my old friend?

Silence.

It is peculiar how sometimes I can hear John's voice in my head and other times I cannot find it.

Now, where were we? I seem to have lost my place.

❧

"Come Mrs. Watson, the game's afoot," I said that night when I arrived, disguised as an American millionaire, at her house.

She looked quite dignified attired as my wife.

I offered her my arm, which she took as we proceeded to the cab I had hired for the evening.

"I've never been to a séance," she said brightly.

I had been to a few, all of which I had revealed as fraudulent. "Well, dear wife, you'll find it most interesting," I answered in my clipped, American accent.

"Hey," she snapped. "It hardly seems fair that just because you're famous you get to speak in a false accent and I don't get to use my Cockney, which I've always been told was quite convincing, Sherlock."

"My name tonight is not Sherlock but Norman Johnson," I answered. "And you may use your accent if it pleases you, Watson."

CHAPTER FOUR

A fraudulent séance (is there any other kind?) is not merely a theatrical exercise, though acting, costumes, lighting, and illusory stage and sound effects are essential. A good séance also requires that a medium interpret and manifest with as much specificity as possible the deep wishes and fears of his or her participants. Also, a séance must seem a proper social occasion, making individuals feel not only welcome but privileged to be included, a rite of aristocratic pomp and particulars, even as it functions at an actual social level that is no more exalted than the shady doings inside a fortune telling wagon at a camp of Romanies. Taking these diverse demands into account, which together make putting on a successful West Side theatrical seem simple by comparison, a good séance might be almost worth the sterling spent on it, authenticity be damned, were it not that at its core is a manipulation of human frailty that preys not on greed, as do most confidence games (whereupon the victim's own failing spells his downfall), but upon grief, victimizing those whose only shortcoming is a broken heart.

"But mightn't Spiritualism, even if false, still sometimes offer comfort for such broken hearts?" Mrs. Watson inquired in response to my dark characterization of the practice.

"*If* false?" I challenged. We were riding in the back of the motor cab from Mrs. Watson's townhouse in Belgrave Square to the home of Madam Du Lac, which was located near St. John's Wood. It was there that the medium offered most of her sittings, including ours tonight (that the séance Conan Doyle had attended was held in the luxurious abode of Lady Vale Owen was an exception). "You must be very clear,

Mrs. Watson, that whatever you see or hear tonight during the séance *is* false. There is no *if* about it. Do not be taken in by mere craft. It is all a trick."

I could not afford for my partner to become bedazzled by whatever lay ahead.

"We're here as investigators," I added. "Not acolytes."

She nodded. "Fine, fine. But you still haven't answered my question, Sherlock. What if Spiritualism, even though it *is* a fraud, is also the only way that some people's grief can ever be eased? Doesn't that give it value?"

"You've a warm heart, Mrs. Watson."

"And you're not answering my question."

I shrugged. "What you suggest is possible. There may be value in deception." After a moment, I attempted to make a joke. "Just consider marriage . . . where would that be without deception?"

Unsmiling, she fired me a sharp look.

"Of course, I'm not referring to your marriage to John," I said, reprimanded.

"I should hope not, Sherlock."

I had planned to further brief her during the motor cab ride on the history of Spiritualism, its practices here and abroad, the societies formed both in support and in opposition to it, celebrated public figures who engaged in the belief, the common techniques and effects of the séance room. But the look on her face suggested that she was already sufficiently briefed.

She was a smart woman, quite capable of following my lead.

So, instead, I reviewed the day's activities to keep her abreast of the case. First, I recounted that morning's more-than-suspicious visit to the Society for Psychic Research; next, I described my afternoon interview of Lady Vale Owen, the dowager who'd hosted the séance that had initiated these events. She had described her interest in Spiritualism as little more than curiosity; however, she admitted the appearance of an "alternate" Stanley Baldwin, a diaphanous, crippled version of our living PM, "took her rather aback." I determined that Lady Vale Owen served no further role in the adventure. The same was true of the handful of other attendees, as well as her servants. Afterward, I called on Conan Doyle, who'd settled himself in my safe house in Bloomsbury. He had taken from my bookshelf a volume of the letters of Cicero, whose prose he admired but whose morality he found somewhat too libertine. Tossing the book aside upon my entrance, he reverted almost immediately to his usual, blustery form, pacing the floor like a caged panther as he complained about feeling a coward for not showing his face on London's streets. So I reiterated to him the necessity of his concealment. Finally I returned to my rooms to prepare my disguise for the séance, and to pack a small bag with make-up and clothing for the different identity I would assume for my midnight appointment at the Society for Psychic Research. "Which brings you up to speed," I said to Mrs. Watson, as the motor cab neared our destination.

"Yes, and now we're on our way to a real séance!" she responded.

I didn't think the words "real" and "séance" belonged in the same sentence but said nothing.

She looked out the window in wonderment.

Her wealth had not changed the fine and humble woman I had known for so long as Mrs. Hudson. We made the rest of the journey in anticipatory silence, broken only when she announced:

"Well *me Deary*, it looks like we're 'ear," in her not unconvincing Cockney accent, as we pulled up to the address I'd given the driver.

I looked at her.

What a retired American millionaire would be doing married to a Cockney woman was beyond me. But I felt quite certain that Madam Du Lac had entertained stranger clients. I wasn't worried about being exposed as a fraud by Madam Du Lac. Rather, it would be the other way around.

I told the cabbie to park across the street, having engaged him for the entire night. After he switched off his motor, I climbed out, walking around the back of the cab to open Mrs. Watson's door.

She took my hand. "Thank you, Norman," she said.

"My pleasure, Emily."

She looked up at me. "That's the first time you've ever called me by my given name and ..." She lowered her voice, "Well, it isn't even me real name. Blimey!"

But that's who we were just then:

Norman and Emily Johnson; he originally from the stylish Nob Hill district of San Francisco, she from the hardscrabble London neighborhood of Stepney, located just a few miles east of this comfortable street but economically and socially about as distant from either St. John's Wood or Nob Hill as the planet Mars. Our contrived history, should we be called upon to recite, was that we'd met while on respective, solitary holidays in Brighton, or, as Norman Johnson would say, "vacations."

In any case, *ain't love strange*?

She wrapped her arm in mine and we started toward the house, which was a red-brick Edwardian, its front garden an explosion of floral color, and its windows alight with a soft, inviting glow. The neighborhood was familiar to me. Thomas Huxley, an acquaintance from the last century, the biologist who became known as "Darwin's Bulldog" for his support of evolution theory, once lived just around the corner (late in Huxley's life, I'd regularly visit his residence, helping him to get the organic-chemical equations correct in his monographs). It was strange to consider that I was now older than Huxley had been when I helped him with his figures so long ago. And he had seemed ancient then.

Surely I had held up to time better than he, hadn't I?

A majordomo welcomed us into the house. He led us through the vestibule and into the sitting room, announcing us to four other couples, all appearing as middle- to upper-class Londoners, who had already gathered in the comfortable environs. Each of our fellow spiritual sitters held a glass of sherry or, in the instances of two teetotaler ladies, dandelion and burdock soda. The Missus and I took sherry and mingled with the others who, unbeknownst even to Mrs. Watson, were all in my employ (more on that later). The light socializing didn't last long before the majordomo returned in what now seemed a role more akin to a Master of Ceremonies.

"If I may please have your attention, ladies and gentlemen," he requested. "An experience of profound mystery and wonder awaits you." His manner bespoke a confidence and dramatic bearing beyond his supposed station in the household. A life in service, which values reserve above all else, does not give a man the ability to switch on such immediate, theatrical verve. I strained my memory. Had I ever seen him before, treading the boards in a West End theater, provincial playhouse, or music hall? (I maintained a mental file of professional actors, as Scotland Yard keeps files on convicts, not so much because theatricals are any more or less honest than others, but because, in my experience, their ability to inhabit roles, their itinerancy, and their not uncommon financial predicaments make them naturals as bit players in the confidence games of professional criminals.) However, I'd not seen this face before. Perhaps he had developed his charismatic manner far from the capital, as the ringmaster of a small circus or as a local politician, both endeavors that serve as criminal breeding grounds even more fertile than life in the theater.

"My name is MacNeil," the majordomo said, his accent localized to this neighborhood. "Welcome to the home of Madam Du Lac, who is presently resting in her boudoir in anticipation of the marvels for which she will soon serve as conduit in the séance room."

I knew this much:

MacNeil, or whatever his real name, was more than majordomo and Master of Ceremonies. Doubtless, he was also Madam Du Lac's séance room collaborator (or one of them). A glance at his attire made that quite certain. I noted his black trousers, which contradicted the pin-striped grey worn by most butlers; even more unconventional was his black jacket, which was of no standard livery cut but more closely resembled a formal, East Indian *sherwani*, akin to the style I had worn that morning, which, when buttoned to the top, would cover him up to his chin, making his attire black from top to bottom. In all, a not unexpectedly exotic outfit for the household of a medium. But fashion was not the point of the subtle variation. While his shoes were well polished, they had rubber soles, enabling him to step silently when called upon to do so. With the addition of black gloves and a black mask, he would become virtually invisible in the darkened séance room, moving about at will, practicing what is known in theatrical circles as the *dark arts*, a stage effect resulting not only in the seemingly inexplicable appearance and disappearance of objects, often coated with radium paint, that seem to float through the darkness in opposition to Newton's laws, but also the brief brushing of one's hair with a breath from a departed loved one, or, assuming the blackened practitioner strong enough or aided by an equally invisible associate, the actual levitation of the medium's chair.

A uniformed policeman entered, carrying a steel lockbox.

MacNeil continued: "The séance room will be quite dark, which, of course, is a requirement of the spirit guide who provides Madam Du Lac access to the 'next world.' We are thereby pleased to provide the services of Thomas B. Keene, a distinguished, off-duty officer of the City of London Police, to personally hold in his certified locked box all of your valuables for the duration of the séance, thereby insuring that in the unlikely event a pickpocket ever slipped into the darkness among our guests, your personal items would be safe."

An impressive maneuver . . . throwing the suspicion of corruption on us. I almost wanted to applaud.

Next, each of the guests was provided a small velvet bag into which we dutifully placed watches, jewelry, billfolds, and whatever personal items we could not bear to lose (which included the photographs of "lost ones" we'd been instructed to bring). Finally, MacNeil asked us to jot on a piece of paper the name of one who had "passed over" and a brief question we would like to ask him or her. These too we placed into our velvet bags, all of which were then locked in the steel box that sat now in the lap of Officer Keene, who had taken a chair near the front door and looked to all the world as reliable a bobby as ever wielded a truncheon.

Of course, this was no scheme to steal our valuables.

How could a spiritual medium build a reputation on such gross criminality?

Rather, the steel box would be opened by the as-yet-unseen Madam Du Lac immediately after we made our way into the séance room and the bags quickly and skillfully rifled for information, providing all that a skilled medium would need to know about her audience to make the wondrous also seem personal. It was a well-managed production, even if the clues to its corruption were evident before the séance began . . . evident, at least, to one with a doubtful mind. But therein lies the rub. People do not attend séances to look for tears in the fabric of Spiritualism's credibility. They go to commune with their lost loved ones. And, for most, what chance does rationalism stand against that?

Officer Keene made a great, silent show of slipping the key to the lockbox into the breast pocket of his uniform and then buttoning the pocket closed, as if that indicated a level of security equivalent to the guarding of the Crown Jewels.

"Has anyone questions?" the majordomo MacNeil inquired.

"Are we to join hands at the table?" asked a woman in a mink stole.

I had instructed my operatives, who filled the room, to approach the séance with whatever curiosity they naturally brought to it. After all, there is nothing like authenticity to stand in for *authenticity* (admittedly, this is a sentence that will make sense only to readers who bring to it a personal understanding of guile and deceit).

MacNeil nodded. "The joining of hands serves two purposes. First, and most importantly, it focuses the psychic energy of the group, making the whole greater than the sum of its parts."

"You're saying that *we* possess psychic energy?" asked a tall woman of advancing years (that is, about two decades my junior).

I gave her a subtle wink, indicating *good question.*

These balding, pot-bellied men and matronly, proper women, posing now as bereaved believers, were no ordinary group of hired operatives. Rather, they all had worked for me years before when, as children or adolescents, they had served as my "Baker Street Irregulars." Starting with six dirty little scoundrels, I eventually created a structured system, rather like a Cambridge University of the streets; as the eldest "graduated" they'd be replaced by new recruits. I'd maintained contact. Yesterday, to a man and woman, they had been delighted to be summoned one more time. In the intervening decades, some had gone on to careers as bankers or businessmen or newspaper reporters, having gained from my assignments and tutelage a sufficient understanding of the malleability of identity to have passed themselves off as far more than the street rats as which they would otherwise have been dismissed. I was proud of them. Watson too had found their advancements most gratifying. Of course, my early training also had made quite adequate criminals of a few, though I can say with pride that none were murderers, rapists, or armed robbers. Tonight, in this room, there was an almost even split between the lawful and the others.

I trusted them all.

"Yes, psychic energy is life energy," MacNeil said in answer to my bejeweled agent's question. "Everyone possess it. Haven't we all had moments of precognition? Or dreams that reveal secrets? Where do you think that comes from? Of course, few are able to channel their psychic energy all the way to the next world, as Madam Du Lac does. She is one in a million. One in ten million! However, your combined energy and faith *does* help her to manage such miracles of inter-world communication."

"And the second purpose of joining hands?" asked a military retiree in formal dress, the left breast of his jacket veritably jangling with medals. I'd known him decades before as Wiggins, who'd served as the motley crew's chief.

"I'm afraid this second reason is far more mundane," MacNeil acknowledged. "But, unfortunately, ours is a cynical world. The joining of hands also serves to assure all participants that no one seated around the table can participate in any sort of trickery whatsoever."

A man once known among the Irregulars as Twist, in homage to the Dickens character, but now looking more like Dickens's respectable Mr. Brownlow, with gold spectacles and a bottle-green coat, commented without irony: "Sadly, ours *is* an age of cynicism."

Meanwhile, across the room, a young woman (the daughter of a former Irregular) who sported bobbed hair, a short, tubular dress, and a cigarette in a long handle, gently touched with her free hand a two foot tall ceramic jar that was set in a line with three others on a wooden altar table. Each of the jars was sealed by a different sculpted head, specifically that of a human being, a jackal, a baboon, and a falcon.

The copper Keene pointed to her but said nothing. He was the muscle. The majordomo was the talker.

MacNeil turned toward her. "Ah, you've discovered the ancient Egyptian canopic jars."

She pulled her hand away as if she ought not to have touched them.

He smiled to reassure her. "Oh, such a light, feminine touch cannot damage them. However, they *are* originals from the Nineteenth Dynasty, specifically the reign of Ramses the Great. More than three thousand years old. So please don't pick them up." As he stepped toward the jars, our attention moved with him. "Such jars as these were used in ancient Egypt to store internal organs of the dead and were buried along with the mummified bodies." His manner betrayed a practiced disquisition. "The sculpted heads atop the jars represent the four sons of the Egyptian god Horus."

I had noted the ancient looking pieces upon entering the room. They were not originals but well-crafted counterfeits. In the majordomo's brief discourse, he had misdated the fake jars, as the use of sculpted stoppers had been discontinued by the time of Ramses the Second.

But I wasn't here to correct him.

Rather, I was here to seem impressed, like the other attendees.

"Do these ancient Egyptian objects hold particular, psychic significance for Madam Du Lac?" asked the former Wiggins, tonight known as Major Angus Spratt.

MacNeil nodded. "What ties Madam Du Lac to these particular jars, which, incidentally, were acquired for her from the Egyptian National Museum by a grateful admirer, is that the Madam's spirit contact is, as some of you may already know, the Pharaoh Ramses the Second himself, whose internal organs remain sealed *in these very jars.*"

All were appropriately impressed.

I was more than merely impressed, but not as MacNeil would have it. Rather, I admired the bold showmanship. In the years since Howard Carter's ballyhooed discovery of Tutankhamen's tomb, Egyptology had become wildly popular throughout England, in fashion, cinema, art, and fiction. Why not incorporate it into a Spiritualist's presentation?

The intestines of Ramses II in a jar? First rate!

"But now we must return to matters of immediate importance," MacNeil said, turning away from the "antiquities."

We gathered more closely around him.

"Are there any among you who suffer from a heart condition? Visitations from the dead can be overpowering, and we wouldn't want to add anyone to the next world prematurely, eh?"

No one suffered from a heart condition.

Next, he asked, "Are there any among you who propose to enter the séance room with intentions that might conventionally be described as being more aligned with the 'demonic' than the 'angelic'?"

From the majordomo's perspective, I suspect that included all of us.

But none of us raised our hands.

"Good," he said.

At this, he opened a set of double doors through which we could see a long hallway that led to another set of double doors.

MacNeil led us down the hallway to the second set of doors.

These opened into the darkened séance room, into which we moved silently.

❧

Madam Du Lac was a woman of beauty and talent. When slumped "unconscious" in her chair, sometimes for up to five long, silent minutes during the séance, she seemed a mere wisp; yet, when "possessed" by her Egyptian spirit guide, she transformed, becoming sinewy, yellow-eyed, and seemingly capable of pharaonic violence. She'd have been a successful medium even if her séance had not been a marvel of stagecraft and new technology, which it was. I cannot pretend to have been unimpressed. The room was lit only by a candle, set at the center of the round table; sometimes, the candle flickered out, leaving us in total darkness, whereupon shimmering objects personally associated with our "departed ones" seemed to appear out of the ether, levitating, only to disappear a moment later, and the powerful male voice of Madam Du Lac's spirit guide, Ramses II, emanated not only from her lips but from various locations in the darkened room, including the ceiling, under the table, and, most impressively, in mid-air, delivering individualized messages to our hand-holding congregation, including Mr. and Mrs. Norman and Emily Johnson, in a strange language that combined English, Egyptian Arabic, Coptic, and an unrecognizable but ancient-sounding tongue, which, I presume, was intended to stand for the unknown pronunciations of the pharaoh's Egyptian, thereby serving to catalogue the entire linguistic history of Egypt, sometimes in a single sentence. Nonetheless, what should have been gibberish proved just exotic enough to *seem* supernatural while still remaining sufficiently coherent to provide the usual vaguely optimistic, from-beyond-the-grave answers to the questions we had written in the parlor and deposited in the lockbox. A well-crafted linguistic stunt that went admirably beyond the minimum requirements of a successful séance. And then, just as suddenly, the candle would relight, seemingly of its own, and in the renewed silence we would discover Madam Du Lac unconscious once more, her head tipped back, but now haloed by clouds of ectoplasm that seemed to emanate from her mouth, rippling above her as if in a breeze, though we felt no movement of air where we sat. Was the ectoplasm taking the three dimensional shape of a face from one of the photographs also included in the lockbox? Yes, a face, ten feet high.

Oh, I could describe additional elements of the production, but, beyond simply establishing the exemplary competence of the sitting, which I believe the previous paragraph accomplishes, to further detail such "wonders" seems a waste of ink, particularly as the most dramatic moment actually occurred when I removed the army-surplus flare I had strapped to my calf and lit it, thereby illuminating the room, capturing *in flagrante delicto* the two men dressed head to toe in black, each with a bag of props slung over his shoulder, looking like a pair of soot covered Father Christmases, and in their free hands short wave radio speakers, their bodies tangled in wires. Madam Du Lac remained in character, "losing consciousness" in the sudden illumination. Meanwhile, the ten-foot-high sculpted ectoplasm that had shimmered above her was now revealed to be a back-lit silk sheet suspended by dozens of tiny, intricately placed strings to produce the three dimensional effect of a face that I doubt the Palace Theatre could manage as cleverly. I understood how a man such as Conan Doyle, intelligent but naturally inclined toward the imaginative (consider his novel about still-existent dinosaurs, *The Lost World*), could have been fooled by the skillful ministrations of Madam Du Lac and her capable assistants.

By now, everyone at the table was standing.

Officer Keene burst through the double doors, a pistol drawn. His expression indicated that he'd never encountered a situation like this.

I turned to him. "What are you going to do, shoot all of us?"

He considered. "I might just have to."

One of Madam Du Lac's assistants removed his black balaclava, revealing his face. It was the majordomo MacNeil. "Put the gun away, Keene," he said, indicating with a nod of his head the weapons in the hands of three of my conspirators at the table, including the jewelry bedecked matron.

The muscle did as he was instructed.

At last, Madam Du Lac opened her eyes, the only one still sitting. She spoke in her own voice, but with a vehemence that her physical fragility belied. She pointed at me, undaunted, fire in her eyes. "You are the devil. I deny you! Your wiles have turned a true Spiritualist experience into a travesty, into the *illusion* of fraud. Prince of liars, get thee back to hell!" She looked at the others gathered around the table. "Do not be deceived by the evil magic of this unbeliever. All is altered. The seeming tricks you see around you are not mine, but Satan's illusions, turned against me to destroy my reputation because of the heavenly blessings I bring to the world."

Ah, the backstage machinery and the black-clad assistants were illusions of the devil . . . She was asking us to disbelieve our lying eyes. When all is lost, invoke Satan, human frailty, and then deny, deny. It had worked before, for thousands of years. It still worked, every day, in nearly every human endeavor. I admired her seeming earnestness, her professionalism. What sangfroid!

"You are both talented and tenacious," I said to her. "Please accept my compliments, Madam Du Lac. But you may dispense with the infernal explanations, as no one here believes you." I moved the flare in a slow circle to highlight the others standing about the table. "They all work for me."

She noted the nods and grins of my former Irregulars. Only then did she come out of character, turning her leonine head to me with a begrudging smile. "So, what do you want from me, Sherlock Holmes?"

I was taken aback. How could she know?

Fortunately, before I revealed my surprise, I realized that she was using the name in jest, as a generic reference to any private investigator or detective. She considered me *a* Sherlock Holmes. The realization came as a relief, despite the accompanying thought that it meant I had lost the proprietary use of my own name, which, apparently, had entered the lexicon as a type.

"Who are you?" she asked.

"Sherlock Holmes," I answered without hesitation, doing away with the American accent.

"And her?" she asked, indicating Mrs. Watson. "That's Watson, I suppose."

"As a matter of fact, yes. I am Holmes and she is Watson."

Madam Du Lac sighed at my apparent unwillingness to come clean about my true identity (the whole world "knew" that Holmes was long retired).

"What do you want me to do, Madam Du Lac?" asked the faux copper, stepping further into the room, his hand still on the revolver.

"Be quiet and put the gun away, Keene," she told him. Then she turned to me. "So, you've come to ruin me?"

"Not necessarily."

She indicated with a wave of her hand the roomful of witnesses to her deceit. "Well, it seems you have."

I shook my head. "If, Madam Du Lac, you agree to answer *truthfully* a few of my questions, which involve matters of far greater import than mere charlatanism, then my agents gathered here will keep private the revelation and techniques of your fraudulence, thereby allowing your spectacular theatrical to continue, as well as the 'donations' you receive from your wealthy, deluded clientele."

"Questions?" she inquired.

In the next few minutes, I dismissed and thanked my Irregulars (quite the reunion), who took with them Madam Du Lac's two black-clad assistants and the disarmed Officer Keene for an enforced night of drinking or opium smoking or whatever might be necessary to render her duplicitous trio unconscious until morning. Meanwhile, Madam Du Lac, Mrs. Watson, and I settled ourselves comfortably in the parlor, where our humbled but still spirited hostess insisted on opening a good bottle of wine to toast our agreement.

The wine proved excellent. (Both Mrs. Watson and I watched Madam Du Lac drink first, to insure that the grape was not of a poisonous character.)

When I complimented the vintage, she smiled.

"The Château Lafite Rothschild, 1881, was paid for by the 'wealthy, deluded clientele' to whom you so recently alluded," she said. "They can afford it. After all, I don't do sittings for paupers. Besides, my well-heeled clients get their money's worth. More, actually."

When I failed to accede, she continued: "Perhaps you misunderstand what I do, sir. My clients leave my séances with newly found peace of mind, often about terrible losses they've endured. Indeed, a peace of mind they'd likely never achieve any other way, regardless of my 'inauthenticity.' So, drink. Enjoy."

"I didn't come here to discuss either the efficacy or the morality of your business, Madam Du Lac."

"Fine, what is it you want to know?"

"I've come here to ask about Stanley Baldwin."

She hesitated. "Our prime minister?" she inquired.

"No, the other one," I said. "The crippled one, from the séance you conducted at the home of Lady Vale Owen."

At this, she looked away. Her complexion paled just perceptibly, a physical effect nearly impossible to consciously manipulate. This, then, was the first genuine vulnerability I had observed in her (even during her chaotic exposure in the séance room she had maintained aplomb).

"Well?" I pressed. "Who put you up to concocting this *other* Baldwin and why?"

She said nothing.

"A man who attended that séance was nearly killed for revealing the strange 'apparition,'" I continued, setting my wine glass on a side table and leaning toward her. "A somewhat distinguished man of letters, quite innocent, perhaps to a fault. Or did you already know about that shooting, Madam Du Lac?"

She shook her head.

"Perhaps you ordered it," I continued.

She looked at me with confusion, but remained silent.

"No," I said, "you haven't the power to make all that has happened, happen."

At this, she closed her eyes. "What's happened?"

"The Society for Psychic Research has been rendered virtually non-existent, or, rather, captured by imposters, without anyone seeming to notice," I answered. "You can't have engineered all that. Who hired you?"

Her continued silence began to irritate me.

"Talk, damn it," I insisted, nearly rising from my seat.

Mrs. Watson put her hand on mine, a subtle exhortation that I soften my approach. Taking her sex into account, I concluded that John's widow might possess insight regarding Madam Du Lac, whose sudden emotional diminishment seemed genuine. So I lowered my voice and sat back on the divan. "I ask myself, Madam Du Lac, what is the logic behind an apparition of a still-living subject, who, apparently, is at once himself and someone else in some 'other' incarnation?

Surely such a visitation breaks with Spiritualist convention. Still, its public exposure oughtn't to be of such alarm that keeping the thing secret would be worth killing for, true?"

Madam Du Lac put her wine glass down. She took a breath before speaking. "My real name is Jane Richardson and I come from Liverpool, where my father was a welder at the shipyards, my mother a fervent believer in Spiritualism, and I an outstanding student of the dramatic arts. I ran away to London at age fifteen in search of stardom in the West End where, instead, I encountered a failed impresario, known to you now as MacNeil, who shortly thereafter became my paramour and partner in crime, which brings us up to the present."

"I didn't ask for a biography," I said.

"It's the truth, which I said I'd give you."

"I don't care who you are. Our agreement was that you answer my questions."

"But that's just it . . . I can't answer what you're asking."

"Why?"

She stood. "The séance at the Vale Owen residence didn't even feature most of the visual effects we produce here," she said. "It was a simple affair, using only the rigged candle, a darkened room, and my assistants moving about, unseen, with the luminescent props. At least, that was the plan. Look, you can ask around the Spiritualist community. I don't engage in the life-sized photographs that some mediums attempt to pass as spirit manifestations. Shoddy. Unreal. You've seen my work. I'm more subtle than that. And I certainly don't produce full-sized, moving, vaguely transparent, *speaking* spirit manifestations. I wouldn't even know how. I wish I did. But that's what appeared in the room, even as I was supposedly in thrall to my Egyptian spirit guide. The thing was real, and I became a mere spectator along with the others. It whispered something into the ear of one gentleman. The writer."

"Real?" I pressed, doubtfully.

"Yes, the spirit of Stanley Baldwin. But crippled, bent about the back and walking with a cane."

I stood, angered by the bald-faced absurdity.

Mrs. Watson, remaining seated, reached up and touched my arm. "Keep calm, Sherlock."

I hadn't lost my temper. I was merely tempted to vehemence.

"Sherlock?" inquired Madam Du Lac, the name by which I prefer to remember her now, rather than the mundane *Jane Richardson* acknowledged moments before. "*Are* you Sherlock Holmes?" she asked.

I said nothing.

Mrs. Watson compounded her mistake by whispering to me, just loud enough to be heard by the medium, "Oh, sorry Sherlock."

I shot Mrs. Watson a glance.

"Yes, you are him," Madam Du Lac said. Fame is a strangely energizing and distracting phenomenon. "I should have guessed," she continued. "Who else could have managed so expertly the disruption in my séance room tonight, afterward dispensing with my assistants as if they were mere children? Oh, Scotland Yard, perhaps. But you're no copper. And you're old enough to be Holmes. Too old to be in this business at all if you weren't him. You can remove that silly moustache now."

I had underestimated my need for adequate disguise. "You're wrong about Scotland Yard," I said.

She looked confused. "You're working for them?"

"No. You're wrong that they could ever have managed as I did tonight."

She shrugged in acknowledgement.

Perhaps in an attempt to atone for her blunder, Mrs. Watson stood and stepped threateningly toward the spiritualist. "Enough of your lying, Missie!"

Quite uncharacteristic.

Madam Du Lac looked at me.

"You can rest easy, Mrs. Watson," I instructed.

Mrs. Watson turned to me. "I was just trying to help."

"Of course," I said. "But I think our work here tonight is done."

"Done?" Mrs. Watson inquired. "But we still don't know who hired her."

"No one hired her," I said. "She's telling the truth."

"What?" Mrs. Watson's face betrayed her confusion.

I looked hard at Madam Du Lac. "If ever you reveal that Sherlock Holmes was here or that I have in any way been involved in this case, I will immediately instruct my agents to publicize the details of your trickery and deceit in the séance room. You will first be a newspaper scandal and shortly thereafter a convicted felon. In short, I will destroy you. Do you understand?"

"I understand."

"Well, I don't," Mrs. Watson said. "Sherlock, are you suggesting that the crippled spirit who appeared to Conan Doyle was real?"

❧

Lest you toss these pages across the room in outrage, allow me to assure you that I was not suggesting the apparition that appeared to the gathering some weeks prior at the residence of Lady Vale Owen was real. At least, not in the sense that Mrs. Watson's question implied. Nor in the manner of Conan Doyle's interpretation. In short, I had not suddenly become an adherent of Spiritualism, which, to this day, I consider to provide no greater channel to mysterious shores than any other human endeavor, including crossing the street or standing in line to post a letter; however, by merely acknowledging the possible existence of mysterious shores I am breaking faith yet again with Dr. Watson's dictum that a narrative be told in chronological order. After all, while standing in the parlor of Madam Du Lac's fashionable home in St. John's Wood, such possibilities were not yet among my thoughts. Rather, I'd simply concluded that Madam Du Lac's denial was truthful because I'd observed none of the seventeen tiny facial impingements I have catalogued as subconsciously occurring, singly or in groups, whenever one lies; additionally, I'd realized that she possessed neither the resources nor the knowledge to have accomplished such an illusion (particularly away from her "rigged" home) and, since deception was her only true area of expertise, she was therefore useless as an agent to whatever more powerful villain lay behind the mysterious incitements.

"We're off," I said to Mrs. Watson.

I had my midnight appointment.

"So, do you think we're on the right track now, Sherlock?" Mrs. Watson asked as we settled into the back of the motor cab.

I nodded.

"But you're not going to let me in on any of your conclusions?" she continued.

"That's right, my dear. Not yet."

She smiled, settling for my diversion.

How often had I employed just such maneuvers with John, which he faithfully interpreted and later depicted in his chronicles as my being one or more steps ahead, my playing coy or laying a trap, when, in truth, it was occasionally the case, as now, that I simply found myself deluged with questions and, temporarily, felt no better equipped to discover their answers than were the court jesters over at Scotland Yard? But I had learned the prudence of withholding one's doubts and questions, even at the risk, or, sometimes, to the purpose, of misleading one's partner, especially when he is your most admiring friend and chronicler. Was it the American writer Mark Twain who said, "It is better to keep your mouth shut and appear stupid than to open it and remove all doubt"? John's ever-allegiant assumptions and subsequent affirmatory chronicles long ago insured that when I kept my mouth shut I appeared anything but stupid, my silence seeming instead a profound, rich, and knowing contemplation. However, don't misunderstand: most often, my silences on cases with John *were* profound, rich, and knowing. It's just that, well, sometimes . . .

From the front seat of the motor cab, idling outside Madam Du Lac's house, the driver turned back to me and asked, "Where to, governor?"

Mrs. Watson looked at me.

"First we drop you at your home," I said to her. "I've a midnight appointment most pertinent to this case."

"Drop me?" The disappointment on her face was evident.

"My dear Mrs. Watson, tonight you proved yourself quite capable at the Great Game. Thank you."

"Sherlock, if your investigation is not yet finished tonight then why should mine be? I'm old, but I'm not tired. Where are we going next?"

"I'm expected alone," I said. "Besides, my meeting will be of a different nature than what we just experienced."

"You mean more dangerous?"

I nodded.

"No matter," she answered, dropping herself into the corner of the back seat as if the decision had been made. "I was made for danger."

"You've read one too many penny dreadfuls, Mrs. Watson." I looked at my wristwatch. It was already after eleven o'clock, which was somewhat later than I thought. I doubted I had time to drop Mrs. Watson at her home and still make my appointment at the Society for Psychic Research. And I daren't be late. "You will wait in the cab nearby," I said. "I will undertake my actions alone but will rejoin you after they're completed. It ought not to take long. And that is nonnegotiable, my dear."

A small smile appeared on her lips. "I suppose that will do."

I leaned toward the driver. "Take us to Hyde Park, near the Palace Green."

The driver nodded, and we started away.

I removed a leather bag I had left on the floor of the cab, and then I turned to Mrs. Watson. "Now, if you would be so kind as to avert your eyes, I must eschew dignity and change clothes here in the cab to prepare for my next meeting. It would not do to show up looking like an American millionaire."

She made a show of turning her head.

But it wasn't modesty that motivated my request.

It was that I did not want her to see me remove John's old service revolver along with the ragged clothes.

CHAPTER FIVE

Having exited the cab near Kensington Square Garden, where I'd instructed the driver and Mrs. Watson to await my return, I approached the Eldon Road offices of the Society for Psychic Research. It was ten minutes before midnight. In the moonlight, the neighborhood, which by day had bespoken only tidy prosperity, now seemed composed of shadowed, landscaped spaces, where, potentially, countless variations on the theme of violence might be concealed. Such is the contextual acuity of perception. I had adopted the guise of an ordinary, professional class Englishman, my appearance altered (a wig and false teeth) only enough to conceal my identity as the most famous consulting detective in the world. After all, it was Siddhartha Singh who'd claimed to have had a séance experience akin to Conan Doyle's. It was he for whom they'd be lying in wait. I had no intention of being shot from a distance. So, as I walked toward the house, I made a point to move with seemingly unguarded ease, a slightly intoxicated sway to my gait, betraying nothing of my defensive attitude.

I'd slipped the revolver into the pocket of my coat.

I stopped on the pavement near the society's office, lighting a cigarette to allow for the possibility that my location was mere coincidence. Casually, I took a long drag and turned in a slow circle, as if taking in both the tobacco and the quiet evening.

The windows of the offices were dark.

This was a strange place for an assault, I thought. An affluent residential neighborhood located a mere stone's throw from numerous embassies, the Natural History Museum, and Kensington Gardens; additionally, there were at least half a dozen houses on the block through whose windows any resident might happen to glance and gain an unobstructed view of . . . well, whatever was to occur. However, everything about this newly counterfeited Society for Psychic Research suggested an uncanny boldness and, perhaps, a troubling competence. It would be redundant for me to acknowledge the villain who again came to my mind (perhaps I remained transfixed by his evil genius because in the years after his death no case ever rose to the complexity and challenge of those that came before, at least not until this one).

All was quiet; nothing on the dignified street stirred.

So I turned and walked through the front garden and up the four brick stairs leading to the door of the darkened offices. I did not knock, but instead sat on the top step, facing the street, and took another long, steady draw on my cig.

Yes, I was the mouse tap-tap-tapping at the spring-loaded trap.

Surely, whoever lay in wait for poor Mr. Singh would now have to consider me either the Rajasthani's agent or an insulant Londoner who paid no heed to private property when pausing in his evening constitutional for a smoke, thereby inadvertently mucking up their operation.

Either instance would require a response.

Thereby, I would make a new acquaintance. We would talk.

And I would learn far more from him than he from me.

After another two or three minutes sitting on the stair, my opportunity showed himself.

A tall, blond man rounded the corner, striding at a military pace; he continued up the street toward my position. Dressed in a well-cut suit as fashionable as the houses and *accoutrements* of this neighborhood, he was thick in his chest and arms and moved with the heavy grace of a rugby full-back. He did not look at me or the house on whose doorstep I casually sat even as he drew nearer.

But I knew he saw me.

Arriving at the path that led up to my perch, he made a hard right and approached through the front garden toward me.

I took another long, languorous draw on my cigarette, smiling as I exhaled.

"Lovely evening, mate," I said, slurring my words enough to suggest drunkenness.

His broad shoulders relaxed, just perceptibly. Nonetheless, he drew close enough for me to smell his cologne, *St. Germain Premium Rose Water*, a new brand preferred by British veterans of the Great War who'd made it back to Paris as tourists in the past two or three years. However, he was no ordinary ex-soldier. No more than thirty years old, the hardness in his eyes suggested even more than the hardness of his body that he could still be a one-man expeditionary force. He looked me up and down and seemed to relax further when he concluded that I was merely an old man in his cups.

"Cigarette?" I offered.

"You've got to go," he said, pulling me up by the collar of my shirt. "This isn't your house. And I've an appointment here."

I turned my head and nodded back toward the door, still in his grip. "But the lights are all out. Nobody's home, no harm done. Sit down and have a smoke with me, young man. It's good for you."

That's when he tossed me like a rag doll from the top step into the small flower garden along one side of the walkway.

It was a long way down.

The landing hurt.

Luckily, nothing felt broken. It seemed that at seventy-three I was still sufficiently well put together to remain in one piece. But I didn't like it. My rheumatism was bound to be inflamed. The behavior was rude even for a professional assassin. So I sat up and spat out a mouthful of soil. "You took me by surprise, young man," I called up to him, unsteadily rising to my feet. My back and shoulders ached. But I stayed in character, resuming the slight slur in my speech. "Otherwise, you'd never have gotten the drop on me. So why don't you come down here and we'll settle this like gentlemen?" At this, I planted my left foot forward, pulled my shoulders back, raised my fists, and assumed a boxing stance. Of course, I had no intention of boxing him.

"Just get out of here, old man."

"Come down here and make me go," I said.

He sighed and came down the stairs, stopping in the garden an arm's length from me, his feet planted firmly. "Last warning, old man. I have an appointment. And I'm not going to let you spoil my plans."

He could have knocked me cold with one punch.

But I didn't allow it. Instead, I confused him for a moment. "Is your appointment with Siddhartha Singh?" I asked in my perfect Rajasthani accent. "Well, I am here, at your service."

His expression was comical. But I knew it would change soon enough.

I shot him.

The discharge was barely louder than a clap of hands as I employed a silencer of my own design on the muzzle of pistol, which I'd fired through the pocket of my coat (ruined now).

He fell backward onto the walkway.

I looked around. The street remained deserted.

I knelt over him where he lay. "Don't worry, you'll live," I said. I had taken care to shoot him through the right lung. I am a good shot. "The bullet has passed clean through you, and any surgeon of above average skill should be able to patch you up," I reassured him. "The lung has likely collapsed and your breathing is doubtless difficult, but you'll live. Unless, of course, I leave you here to bleed out."

He didn't look at all happy.

I removed from his jacket pocket the handgun that I felt confident had been used to shoot Conan Doyle.

"At the end of this street is a telephone box from which I will call for an ambulance, dear boy, if you tell me what I want to know," I said. "The ambulance will race to this scene and you will be saved. Or not. Do you understand me?"

His eyes began rolling back in his head.

I slapped him hard a few times to bring him back. "Don't pass out!"

He took heed.

"Who hired you?" I asked.

"You bloody old bastard," he muttered, attempting to spit at me. Quite impressive for one recently shot through a lung.

I stood as if to go. "No phone call."

"Eureka," he said.

"What? Who?"

"The Eureka Society," he managed, gasping between syllables. "That's all I know. Make the call for an ambulance."

I'd never heard of any such group. But I believed him.

So I knelt once more at his side, removed my cotton muffler from my neck, and wound it tightly around his chest to staunch the bleeding. He passed out. I made the call from the red telephone box.

❧

You may be wondering why I did not simply let the assassin die.

The fact is that when one shuffles a professional killer off this mortal coil, one discovers that there is always another to take his place, that there is no end to them. We train young men to be soldiers, teaching them to kill; quite naturally, a small percentage excel at the activity, and a percentage of those will later choose to use their gifts, not for country but for personal gain, absent ethical considerations. Trained killers can always be hired. Permanently removing one from the world is useless. Besides, the point of the night's endeavor was neither revenge nor righteousness but investigation, as I believed that the only way to make Conan Doyle safe was to expose and eliminate the man or organization who had hired the shooter. Just as capturing the king is the goal of chess, the object of an investigation is solving the mystery. I did not let the assassin die simply because to do so in no way served my ultimate purpose (and my simple disguise insured he could hold no personal grudge).

Or . . . perhaps that is not what you're wondering.

Perhaps you're wondering about *me*.

After all, until you picked up these pages, you can't have read a fully authentic account of my work.

Of course, I told you at the start that I am not who you think I am.

Still, misconceptions are no fault of yours. It is reasonable that you may have been surprised by my shooting first and asking questions later in the garden of the Society for Psychic Research.

I have read the American writer Zane Grey, and I have seen moving pictures featuring Tom Mix and William S. Hart, so I understand the popular ethic of the Wild West hero, which has swept Britain just as it has swept much of the world. Firing a weapon at a man is acceptable *only* provided the other has drawn first. But the same has also long been true of the romantic historical novels of Sir Walter Scott or, for that matter, Conan Doyle (swords, guns, what's the difference?). But all that is fiction. Nonetheless, more than forty years ago Dr. Watson adopted much the same ethic in his depictions of our actual cases. This is what I meant when I referred to his use of dramatic license in the published accounts of our adventures. Inevitably, readers grew attached to the conventionally heroic depiction of . . . well, me. I say again that I believe Watson did this with no intention to deceive or even to profit directly from softening his accounts; rather, he simply found it "ungentlemanly" to tell a story any other way. However, the actual business of investigating crime is most ungentlemanly. For example, had I waited for the assassin to draw his pistol before drawing mine, he'd simply have shot me dead and there would be nothing more to tell.

That is how it works in real life.

Does it mitigate matters that I consider it a near certainty that the blond assassin survived the shooting, at worst losing the use of one lung, and that his prognosis is for a complete recovery, excepting occasional shortness of breath? My aim was true. Does that alleviate my having shot him without first having manfully called for him to "Draw!" or "Put your hands up!"? I apologize if I seem disagreeable or even sarcastic on this issue.

But nothing is simple, nothing straightforward.

So, I did not leave the assassin to bleed to death, unattended. But, of course, this means he is now likely to kill again, someone, somewhere, sometime. So is his survival a good thing, sparing me the appellation of *killer*? Or is it a bad thing, making me a kind of conspirator in his next, unforeseen murder?

Good, bad . . .

Allow me to repeat: nothing is simple, nothing straightforward.

Having long ago arrived at this understanding, I resolved that I would value only the playing of *the game*. And I played the game well at the offices of the Society for Psychic Research. I gained a clue: "Eureka," Greek for *I have found it*, made famous by the story of Archimedes in the bath tub. That I was unfamiliar with any such organization mattered little to me just then.

What mattered was that the game was truly begun.

And my mysterious opponent seemed worthy indeed.

⚓

I climbed into the cab where I had left it.

"Heavens, Sherlock!" Mrs. Watson cried as I settled in beside her. She pointed to my shoulder. "Have you been shot?"

I glanced down. My coat was bloodstained where I had brushed against the blond assassin's wound. "No, I'm fine."

"But that's *blood* on your coat," Mrs. Watson whispered.

"It's not mine."

From the front seat of the motor cab, the driver turned back and asked, "Where to, governor?"

"Stay here for a moment, if you please," I answered, curious to see if the ambulance I called would arrive alone or accompanied by some other vehicle.

"What happened?" Mrs. Watson pressed, indicating the blood.

I closed the small window that separated us from the driver.

"Disgraceful behavior," I answered her.

She set her eyes upon me. "On whose part?"

"Don't forget, my dear, that we are the heroes. Not the villains."

"True, but that doesn't answer my question."

"A most insightful commentary."

Being familiar with my methods, Mrs. Watson did not press it further. Instead, she asked, "What did you learn out there?"

"The game's afoot, my dear," I said.

She sighed. "That much I already knew," she said. "In any case, while you were out 'adventuring' I made this list."

She handed me a sheet of paper upon which she had written in careful penmanship the following, numbered questions:

1) Who saw through your expert disguise as Cambridge tutor and why expose the information to Conan Doyle?
2) Why communicate the information to C. D. in such a bizarre manner?
3) Does it matter that the supposed spirit manifestation was of an "alternate" Stanley Baldwin, our current PM? Political? Or might the manifestation have been anyone?
4) How was the effect of the supernatural visitation achieved, since it seems beyond even the formidable techniques of Madam Du Lac?
5) Why shoot C. D.?

"This is very good, Mrs. Watson," I said, folding her list. It *was* good, if incomplete.

"But you're still not going to share *your* theories or conclusions?" she asked.

"What I discovered while 'adventuring' was a sixth question for your excellent list, Mrs. Watson."

She sat up straighter. "Which is?"

"What is the 'Eureka Society'?"

She shook her head. "Never heard of it. What is it, Sherlock?"

"If *I* knew, then it wouldn't be a question for your list," I answered. "And that's quite strange, as I have more than a passing familiarity with secret societies. Hundreds. Thousands. But one's knowledge can never be truly comprehensive. Actually, such omniscience would make life rather tedious, don't you think?"

"I've never had to worry about omniscience," she responded.

"Nor I," I admitted. "Whatever the cinema or theatricals or even some of John's accounts may suggest."

"So how do we find out what this Eureka Society is?"

"Research." I removed my wig and slipped out of my blood stained jacket, stuffing them (along with the gun) back into my bag.

"As at a library?"

"Exactly. Now."

"But the hour ..." Mrs. Watson slid slightly nearer. She lowered her voice as if the driver could hear us. "The library's closed."

"I have associates among the night watchmen," I said.

She smiled. "Of course you do, Sherlock."

The ambulance raced past us, unaccompanied by other vehicles. Still, I knew other wheels were spinning.

I slid open the driver's window: "The British Museum; specifically the library wing," I instructed. "But first we'll drop Mrs. Watson at her home."

The driver started away.

Mrs. Watson looked at me. "I'm *not* tired, Sherlock."

"I'm afraid the next stop will be less engaging than these last two," I explained.

"I'm sure I could be of some help, as I know my way quite well around libraries," she said. "Since John's death I've spent countless days among the stacks at the British Museum. I'm very good now with the Universal Classification System."

"Some of the research I'll be doing will entail an entirely different kind of classification system."

"Dewey Decimal, like the Americans?"

I shook my head. "There is a secret library classification system known only to a few hundred men and women throughout the world, even though the system is employed in many major libraries, always under the very noses of the uninitiated librarians."

"Why?"

"Because some information is essential but too dangerous to make readily accessible. So it is scattered about the stacks in what would seem to be unintelligibly random placements."

"What sort of information?"

"Lists and descriptions of secret societies, both from the past and the present."

"How does the classification system work?"

"It's rather too complicated to explain at one sitting. Besides, I am not at liberty to share the information."

She gave me a hard look.

So I offered to her what I could, as I offer now to you, dear reader: "Suffice to say that the resources are not to be found in any one section but are scattered among books with innocuous titles wholly unrelated to the true subject matter."

"That subject matter being secret societies," she proposed.

"Yes."

"But what if some ordinary patron stumbled upon such a book?" she asked, quite reasonably.

"The information is coded and contextualized so that even in such a case the reader of his or her chosen volume on zoology, astronomy, knitting, or whatever subject, would find the hidden text indistinguishable from the rest."

"Remarkable," she said. "How often have you used such resources in your cases?"

"Occasionally."

"And John knew this 'coded' classification system?"

I shook my head. "The numbers entrusted with the use of such a system are, for obvious reasons, quite small."

"But he knew the resource existed?"

"Actually no," I said.

"Why not? Surely John was trustworthy."

"Indeed he was. I suppose I didn't tell him about the resource because . . ." I stopped.

She waited.

I hadn't an answer that pleased me, so, rather than complete the aborted sentence, I changed the subject. "So, you see, Mrs. Watson, there would be little for you to do at the library. It's far better to get you home."

She shifted in her seat. "What, exactly, do you think awaits me at home?" She didn't allow time for an answer (such as safety, warmth, sleep, etc.) but provided her own. "*Nothing* awaits me there, Sherlock. Nothing but silence."

"A library cultivates silence even during working hours," I observed. "In the dead of night . . ." I allowed the phrase to speak for itself.

"Surely you know there are different kinds of silence."

I knew her reference was to her not wanting to be alone, a vulnerability to which I considered myself immune.

"I could simply find a good book and keep watch in the library," she volunteered. "I'll ensure that no villain sneaks up on you."

I wasn't much worried about my safety in the library.

She touched my hand. "Then, when your research leads you to some amazing conclusion, I'll be the first to know," she said.

"It's late. You've no need to sleep?"

"How many septuagenarians do you know who sleep well at night?" she asked, rhetorically.

I leaned toward the driver. "No need to stop at Belgrave Square, my good man," I instructed. "Just take us both straight on to the British Museum."

He nodded and started for the great edifice in the city center.

She smiled. "Now, about that blood on your jacket . . ." she started.

I held my hand up to stop her. "Enough questions, Mrs. Watson. We'll have much to discuss after I've completed my research."

She nodded. "Fair enough."

However, after hours of my moving alone through the darkened stacks, I had uncovered no information about a "Eureka Society." I'd scanned accounts and even membership roles of hundreds of fraternal orders, "magical" organizations, Pythagoreans, cabals of politicians, criminals, clergymen . . . But nothing brought me nearer my goal.

Was it possible the blond assassin had lied to me, even as he lay bleeding?

Not likely.

At last, wearily, I made my way down from the fourth floor to the library's magnificently domed Reading Room. The vast room was illuminated by the first light of morning streaming through tall windows at the base of the dome. Near the center of the otherwise unoccupied expanse sat Mrs. Watson, her head resting upon her folded arms on a table, an open book face down at her side. Her soft snoring echoed through the space.

I approached and tapped her shoulder. "Mrs. Watson?"

She opened her eyes, taking a moment to gain her bearing. "Oh!" she said as she looked around. "Funny, I was dreaming I was in my bed asleep. But here I am . . . Um, where am I? Oh, the library! Of course. I must look a mess. How embarrassing, my falling asleep in a public place."

"No need for embarrassment," I assured her. "And it's hardly been 'public' these past hours. But now it's morning."

She looked up at the windows. "Yes, I see. How quickly the night went. Did you solve the mystery, Sherlock?"

"Not yet. Nonetheless, it's time we left here."

"Yes, the morning shift will be on soon. All those librarians! We wouldn't want to be caught here after hours. Or, rather, before hours. Or . . . whatever."

"What were you reading?" I asked, as she closed the book on the table before her.

"Poe," she said. "I enjoy his tales of the macabre."

"Poe . . ."

"Yes, Edgar Allan. The American from the last century. Surely, you've heard of him."

Of course, I'd heard of him.

My voice brightened and I felt renewed, as if I had not spent the past hours in fruitless research. "Poe!" I exclaimed. "It might just be . . ." I stopped, turning possibilities over in my head.

"Be what?" she pressed.

I pointed to the book. "It might be that what we're seeking is right there before us."

She looked at me as if I had gone slightly mad. "In Poe's book?"

"Yes. How quickly can you be ready to leave town?"

"Where to?"

"Paris," I said, glancing at my watch. "If we hurry we can catch the 7:54 to Dover to make the crossing!"

"*This* morning?" she asked.

"Indeed," I answered, grabbing the book of Poe from the table to take with me (apologies to the British Library).

"What's in Paris?" she asked.

The most unusual archive in the world, I thought. A reservoir of secrets as explosive as anything found in the great British library, including the specially catalogued materials. However, that's not what I said. "The finest *patisseries*. I could do with a good *croissant*."

She looked at me skeptically. "You're not going to tell me," she observed.

"I'll do better, Mrs. Watson. I'll show you."

In that morning's newspapers, which I bought before we boarded the train at Victoria Station, I discovered further indication of our opponent's formidability. All the papers ran the same inaccurate account of the shooting outside the offices of the Society for Psychic Research. My having called an ambulance, which doubtless arrived with bell clanging, waking every resident of the street to wander out as witnesses, made complete denial of the incident impossible. However, the quoted constabulary attributed the non-fatal shooting to a common robbery; additionally, the illustration of the victim's face was not the blond man I had actually shot. The name of the victim and other information was doubtless false too.

As they say in the American pulps, "the fix was in."

CHAPTER SIX

After disembarking the train in Paris at the Gare Montparnasse, Mrs. Watson and I proceeded by motor cab past the Luxembourg Gardens to the Hotel de la Sorbonne, where we would rest and dine before walking to our ultimate destination, a small, used bookshop in the Saint-Germain-des-Prés district of Paris. On the trip from London, which had taken the entire day, I had, at first, resisted Mrs. Watson's queries about my investigative breakthrough, my "Eureka" moment earlier that morning in the Reading Room, promising her somewhat cryptically, perhaps habitually, that soon all would be made clear; however, in the middle of the Channel her persistence wore me down and, when I discovered she had read only a selection of poems and short stories of E. A. Poe and none of his essays, I recognized that she would benefit from a modest briefing to help her make sense of the next leg of our investigation. I ordinarily saved such disclosures for moments of high, often climactic, drama. Consider the canon of Dr. John H. Watson and the nature of nearly every major revelation contained therein. To share such good material in a mere conversation aboard a cross-channel steamer seemed a waste.

Nonetheless, shipboard, I shared such a hint of my hypothesis with her.

(Was I more inclined to expose my thought processes to Mrs. Watson than I'd have been to John, whose request for "background" I'd have denied under similar circumstances, because she was a woman and therefore more intellectually needful? I reject the suggestion. My regard for the intelligence and formidability of females is far greater than that for which I am popularly given credit. For example, in John's account, "A Scandal in Bohemia," my reference to Irene Adler as *the* woman was not a sign of romantic attachment, as the theatricals now prefer to portray, but an acknowledgement of Irene's intellect and cunning, which matched my own, an estimation I associate now with only one other living being, my wretched, octogenarian brother Mycroft. Or, following in that vein, did I share my thinking with Mrs. Watson because *she* had charmed me in a romantic way? She is indeed a most charming woman. But I can say with pride that during my decades as a consulting detective I have never allowed my actions to be swayed by such passions. Of course, my pride in this fact must be tempered by acknowledgement that when it comes to personal attraction my tastes have always been ephemeral and quite narrow. Narrow almost to the point of nonexistence. [Further discourse on the topic of my personal attractions is beyond the scope of this endeavor.] So, finally, did I offer Mrs. Watson an explanation mid-Channel because she was not my chronicler, and, therefore, I had no dramatic narrative arc to construct simultaneous to solving the mystery at hand, as I had constructed on so many occasions with John? I recall making no such conscious decision. Nonetheless, this may best explain my openness with her.)

Doubtless, Dr. Watson would remark now: *Get back to the story, Holmes. And no more parentheses within parentheses. Ever! Indeed, no more parentheses for you at all.*

Good advice.

However, while I may be the greatest consulting detective the world has ever known, I am but an amateur when it comes to writing, and so I find myself in need of a space break, whether or not such a literary device is justified by this chapter's initial structure, which, I realize, refers to a used book shop in Paris where, it now appears, we will not arrive for at least a few more pages.

Back to that morning's Channel crossing:

Sunlight glimmered on the water as our steamer sliced through gentle swells. It was a good day to be at sea. An hour and a half out of

Dover, the white cliffs remained visible, tiny, in the direction of the stern, and the coastline of France was a vague silhouette ahead.

Mrs. Watson and I occupied deck chairs.

To avoid being recognized back in the crowded port, I had donned a weathered pea coat, a sailor's knit cap, sunglasses, and a false beard, looking every bit the retired sea dog. I remained in the disguise aboard ship as well.

"So, Edgar Allan Poe is a part of this?" Mrs. Watson asked, sliding her chair beside mine until their wooden armrests touched.

"Indirectly, I suspect." I withdrew from my hastily packed over-night satchel the volume of Poe that Mrs. Watson had set spine up on the library table before resting her head on her arms and falling asleep beside the book. "You see, aside from the poetry and gothic fiction for which he is best known, Poe was a critic and essayist. Unfortunately, none of this productivity resulted in financial security during his life-time, and so he began lecturing on a modest circuit. In time, this career maneuver might have led to wider exposure, popular acceptance, and greater resources, except that in 1849 he died under mysterious circum-stances at the age of forty."

"Poor man," Mrs. Watson commented. "Not all authors are as for-tunate as our John when it comes to readership."

Our John. "True," I said.

"But what has this to do with our case?"

"Poe's last major work was a long essay called, 'Eureka,' which is little read now, though he considered it his masterpiece."

"Eureka . . . Like the Eureka Society," she ventured.

"Yes, I should have made the connection immediately," I acknowledged.

She shook her head, smiling tenderly. "Oh, Sherlock, you mustn't be hard on yourself. In our dizzy age, the mind works a tad more slowly than before."

I sat up straighter in my deck chair and turned to face her, removing my sunglasses for emphasis. "I've not found that to be the case, Mrs. Watson. My mental capacities have undergone no diminishment."

"Oh, my apologies."

She looked more chastened than I'd intended. So I softened my remark with a minor fabrication. "Well, perhaps from time to time I have had to reach for a concept that, in the past, was always just *there*."

She smiled in acknowledgement.

I settled back in my deck chair, replacing my sunglasses with my reading glasses and continued with my discourse, opening the book of Poe. "'Eureka' is subtitled 'An Essay on the Material and Spiritual Universe,' which offers a sense of Poe's enormous ambitions. It is uneven in its qualities, though not without interest. Indeed, fascination. Particularly in light of recent events." I rifled the pages. "Poe suggests here that 'space and duration' share the same essence, anticipating Einstein by many decades. And he makes numerous other cosmological assertions of varying validity." I found the passage I sought. "Of interest to our case, Mrs. Watson, is the following assertion. It reads as follows: 'Let me declare that there does exist a limitless succession of Universes, more or less similar to that of which we have cognizance.'"

I closed the book.

"'Limitless succession of universes'?" Mrs. Watson queried. "What does that mean? Universes occurring one after the other?"

I shook my head. "Rather, all occurring at once."

"Was he mad?"

I shrugged. "He was possessed of certain characteristics and habits that medical experts too often carelessly label as 'mad,' but that does not mean his ideas were less cogent than those of any other genius."

She looked puzzled. "So, what does he mean by 'limitless Universes'?"

I spent the next few minutes outlining Poe's counterintuitive notion of innumerable, autonomous worlds existing simultaneous and parallel to our own. No mere metaphors. Universes as real as ours, if unknowable. Further, I explained that while most of these worlds must be wildly divergent from ours, the mathematics of incalculably vast numbers necessitates that many would be like our own, populated by variations of ourselves and others that we know. Or so Poe's notion dictated.

She looked at me as if I were mad. "That's the stuff of fiction, Sherlock. Not fact."

I had to admit it sounded far more like the fantasies of H. G. Wells than the reasoned workings of Newton.

"Poe argues this case convincingly?" she asked.

"Poe's logical inferences are not without flaw. Nonetheless, he was possessed of an inquisitive and often insightful imagination."

"And he conceived this out of whole cloth?" she asked.

"There were precursors," I said. "I can think of a few. Giordano Bruno was burned at the stake by the Church in 1600 for his 'heretical' book, *On the Infinite Universe and Worlds*. Anaxagoras of Clazomenae modeled a universe in which all possible worlds exist, openly questioning why there should be only one universe. And you'll find further similar conjecture in the works of Epicurus, Lucretius, the Stoics, Nicholas of Cusa, and others."

"But Poe is of the modern era," Mrs. Watson observed.

"Relatively speaking."

"How does this relate to our case?"

"Consider," I suggested. "'Limitless universes more or less similar to that of which we have cognizance.'"

She narrowed her eyes, perplexed.

"Mrs. Watson, allow me to set aside all ordinary good sense, in addition to discarding the scientific method, and ask a question in the interest of . . . well, let's call it intellectual exercise."

"Go ahead."

"Mightn't 'limitless universes' account for the existence of more than one Stanley Baldwin?"

She worked through it aloud. "You mean one Baldwin who was crippled at twenty-nine, and another who avoided such a fate and is now our prime minister?" She didn't wait for an answer but shook her head. "It's impossible. You, of all people, can't believe such a thing."

"Oh, I don't *believe* anything," I answered. "Faith is a virtue I abjure. However, in this instance, belief may occupy a central role. Not *my* beliefs, which are nil. Rather, what interests me is what others may believe and the actions that such belief may inspire."

"Actions, such as shooting poor Conan Doyle?" she asked.

I nodded.

"And who are these others?" she pressed.

I opened my palms to indicate that I didn't yet know.

She looked confused.

I didn't blame her, as I was on uncertain ground myself.

I watched her gather thoughts before she asked, "How would such a visitation from an alternative world even occur?"

"I can offer no answer."

"Then at least tell me this. Why are we going to Paris? And please don't say *haute cuisine*."

"We're going to Paris because of mysterious circumstances surrounding Poe's death seventy-nine years ago."

"What circumstances?"

"Well, that's just it. Beyond being 'mysterious' I don't know."

"*You* don't know?"

I did not rise to the bait. "Poe's case has never before intersected with a relevant investigation of my own. But now that it may . . . well, answers await."

"And these 'circumstances' may relate to Poe's theory of limitless universes and, thereby, to our case?"

"Perhaps."

"Poe died in Paris?"

"No," I answered. "In America. Baltimore."

"Then why . . . ," she started.

I held up one hand, settled back in my deck chair, and closed my eyes. It had been a long time since I'd slept. And, as I noted before, I'd already provided her with far more explanation than was my habit. "Let's leave some of what's to come as a surprise," I suggested. "What do you say to that, Mrs. Watson?"

I didn't hear her answer.

Perhaps she said nothing. Or perhaps sleep overtook me just then.

Hours later, Mrs. Watson and I checked into rooms in the modest and inconspicuous Hotel de la Sorbonne, where we changed out of our traveling clothes and I donned my ordinary apparel, sans disguise. I've discovered these past years that when I'm on the continent my advanced age makes me virtually unrecognizable, even to the fans of true crime who'd likely recognize me in England, their expectations unconsciously informed by geographical context. This near-assurance of anonymity is even more pronounced in Paris than in other European capitals, as the rare Parisian who does recognize me invariably turns away without acknowledgement, his national pride threatened by the mere sight of an *English* consulting detective who, these days, is more renowned than their own great sleuth from the last century, Le Chevalier C. Auguste Dupin.

More about Dupin shortly.

By the time Mrs. Watson and I left the hotel, the cafés were crowded with hungry diners, *apéritifs* long finished, *vin ordinaire* being poured; Mrs. Watson and I had eaten lightly at our hotel, so we made our way without culinary interruption through the small, winding streets that led out of the Latin Quarter; we dodged motor cars as we emerged onto the Boulevard Saint-Michel near where it crosses the Boulevard Saint-Germain, which we followed all the way to Rue des Saints-Péres.

"Lovely city, especially at night," Mrs. Watson observed.

"Yes, if you like that sort of thing," I answered, pushing forward along the pavement.

"What's not to like about loveliness?" she asked, working to keep up with me even as she attempted to take in the architecture, the horse chestnut trees, the chic fashions in shopfront windows, the sonorous fragments of *bal-musette* music, sometimes carefree, sometimes bittersweet, that emanated from bustling cafés, the young, passing faces of varied nationalities, many of whom bore expressions either of wonder, akin to Mrs. Watson's, or its opposite, the ennui associated with the city's sophisticates.

"Frankly, I prefer London, Mrs. Watson."

"Why?"

"The grime," I answered.

When we reached Rue des Saints-Péres we turned toward the river and proceeded for several minutes; here, it was shadowy and quiet, every business shuttered for the night. "We've arrived," I said, stopping before the one shopfront that was not shuttered, a darkened, used bookshop that bore on its door a hanging sign that read *Fermé*.

"Closed," Mrs. Watson muttered. "Looks like we'll have to come back tomorrow."

I shook my head no. The shopfront window bore the shop's name in faded paint:

Le Rossignol
Livres D'Occasion

Beside the words on the glass was an equally neglected painting of the shop's namesake, a nightingale perched on the long stem of an ornately decorated, old-fashioned key.

"Before we discuss the name of this august institution, please observe the books displayed in the window," I instructed Mrs. Watson, who moved beside me and put her head almost to the glass.

A nearby streetlight cast just enough light.

She turned first to the left and then stepped slightly to the right, taking in the entire, display. Then she looked up at me. "Nothing very special as far as I can see. Of course, I am no bibliophile. Am I missing something?"

"Not at all," I assured her. "Indeed, you've captured the essential characteristic of the display. It includes not a single first edition. Nor, if I may be allowed an Americanism, are there any former 'bestsellers.' Nor is there even one copy of a cheap school edition of a classic. And look at the biographies. Have you heard of any of those books' subjects?"

Again, she squinted through the glass, silently mouthing the names of the biography subjects. She shook her head.

"Nor I," I admitted.

She turned to me surprised. "*You've* never heard of any of them?"

"Please, Mrs. Watson, I acknowledge my ignorance of the subjects of these biographies not as a show of humility but as evidence of the relative insignificance and subsequent disinterest the lives of these men bear even for those invested in a wide variety of subjects, such as myself. In short, there is nothing in this window display that would be deemed worthy even of the *bouquinistes*, the book stalls along the Seine, where, incidentally, a collector *can* occasionally find valuable editions."

"So how does the display attract customers?" she asked, reasonably.

"It doesn't."

After a moment of confusion, an expression crossed her face as of sudden and delighted comprehension. "Ah, I think I have it! Do the books formulate some kind of message or code?"

I shook my head. "The display is nothing more than a selection of books that will never appeal to any reader."

"So how does the shop do business, Sherlock?"

"The purpose of the shop is not business."

"Then what is it? How does the shop stay open?"

"The shop is never open, though I suppose you could say it's never actually closed either, despite the sign hanging on the door."

She stepped past me to the door and attempted to turn the handle. It was locked. She turned back to me with an expression that was both curious and vaguely impatient. "Well, Sherlock, it's closed now."

I nodded in acknowledgement of her experimental method. Then I pointed to the shopfront window and the name and illustration thereupon. "The Nightingale," I said.

Now her impatience was turning to frustration. "Thank you, Sherlock. But I speak a little French myself."

"Do you think it a suitable name for a used bookshop?"

"As suitable as any other, I suppose," she answered.

I concurred. "Now, look at the illustration."

She did as I asked. "Yes, a nightingale perched on a key."

"Exactly," I said. "And there you have it."

She hesitated, as if I were going to say more. When I didn't, she shrugged. "What do I have?" she asked. "I don't understand." However, before I could offer the ingenious answer, she continued. "Frankly, Sherlock, I don't know how John put up with these kinds of cryptic maneuvers for all those years. What kind of partner are you anyway? I mean no offense, but . . . you ask me one question after another, when you might just tell me why we're here and what this place is."

I was prepared to concede the point.

However, Mrs. Watson wasn't finished. "I used to wonder how John kept from punching you in the nose back in the Baker Street days. Oh, I was merely the landlady, serving tea from time to time. Still, I observed how you used your intellect with John."

"And how was that?"

"You used it in a . . . well, a *superior* manner."

"I'm afraid I used it that way with everyone."

"Yes, but John wasn't 'everyone.'"

"That's true."

"I always knew he admired you," Mrs. Watson continued, her tone softening. "Everyone did, does . . . But for him to have been so patient with you. For *so long*. Admiration alone is not enough. Nor was the privilege of accompanying you on your adventures. Nor the chronicling of them. Nor even the profit from the publications, which he never expected you to insist he keep entirely for himself. Money didn't matter to him. So what does that leave? Only this. He must have truly liked you, Sherlock."

"Of course he did," I answered without hesitation. This was not how I had envisioned our arrival here at Le Rossignol, the next important step in our investigation. I had looked forward to revealing to her marvelous secrets about this place. Nonetheless, here on this dark, deserted street, the topic of conversation had changed, seemingly of its own accord. Of course, I knew it was actually Mrs. Watson's doing, facilitated by the natural capacity of her sex to maneuver conversation. So I attempted to acknowledge her premise in a straightforward manner, hoping we could then return to the critical matters at hand, to our *raison d'etre*. "John liked me just as I liked him."

But she was not finished.

Instead, she looked at me as if searching for something specific. Then her expression warmed. "I know you liked him, Sherlock. Truly, I do. But, perhaps, the way you liked him was not quite the same as he liked you."

I wasn't sure how she meant this. "Look, are we working on a case here or aren't we, Mrs. Watson?"

She smiled, ignoring my provocation. "*I* like you, Sherlock. I always have. Otherwise, I'd never have put up with you as a tenant. Surely, you gave me grounds to evict. And I'm not saying John wasn't right to like you as well. Why, I'd go so far as to say he was right even to have loved you, despite your . . ." She stopped, searching for a word.

I waited.

"Despite your . . ." she repeated, still searching for the word.

"My arrogance?" I suggested.

She shook her head.

"Egotism?"

She considered longer this time, but again shook her head.

"Pride?"

"Oh, that's one of the Seven Deadly Sins," she observed. "Let's not get carried away, Sherlock. You're not *that* bad, whatever you may think. I'm just talking about your capacity for . . . oh, what you're doing to me here tonight with all these blasted questions." Her eyes brightened when she discovered the word she wanted, "Fastidiousness. Yes, your fastidiousness!"

I nodded in acknowledgement.

"Is 'fastidiousness' a word?" she asked.

"It is," I said.

She turned back toward the window. "So, please explain to me in *as straightforward a manner as possible* how this shop's window, featuring nothing of value, figures in the case, how this shop can be at once both never open and never closed, and, finally, what the name of this strange business and the supposedly apt image of this nightingale means, if you please."

CHAPTER SEVEN

The book shop's name, Le Rossignol, and accompanying image of a nightingale perched on a key, alluded not only to a bird but, more significantly, to a slang term popular among burglars in the last century for a key that would open any door, what we commonly refer to as a "skeleton key." In this unusual instance, "the nightingale" that unlocked the door to this shop was no specific key, but *any* key, insuring that the establishment could be entered at any time by anyone with knowledge of what lay inside. Of course, few possessed such knowledge.

Indeed, it may be that I alone was ever so informed.

"Go ahead, Mrs. Watson, try your key," I instructed.

The shop neither sold books nor entertained customers but, instead, served as a repository of some of the most sensitive secrets and historical artifacts of the French state, specifically, the numerous unpublished cases of my great predecessor in the art of detection, C. Auguste Dupin. Eight decades earlier, he had investigated a case involving Edgar Allan Poe. I had read many of Dupin's cases, but not this one, as it had held no specific relevance.

"What key?" Mrs. Watson asked.

"Your hotel room key."

She gave me a quizzical look.

"Just try it," I instructed.

A moment later she turned to me with wonder. She'd unlocked the locked door. "But how did you come to know about this, Sherlock?"

"Let's go inside," I said.

In the early 1890s, after I'd gained international fame, I received a caller at Baker Street who was then about the age I am now; he requested from me no professional consultation but, instead, had come to share the existence of the used bookshop on Rue des Saints-Pères, as well as its secret purpose and means of access. As you may have surmised, the visitor was C. Auguste Dupin. Naturally, I was pleased to receive so celebrated a figure. Dr. Watson was away that day, which was surely no accident, as Dupin was deliberate in all his undertakings. His handshake was firm, but his health was clearly quite poor. I was forty years his junior; however, he spoke to me as an equal, though, being French, he could not resist asserting that if the word "detective" had existed in common usage in the middle years of the last century, the years that coincided with his most famous investigations, he'd have gained international fame at least equal to mine. Of course, I knew it was more than mere vocabulary that explained our discrepancy in the public's imagination, and I humbly asserted as much. There was, for example, his anonymous chronicler, who, unlike my dear Dr. Watson, had permitted only three of Dupin's cases ever to come to print, entrusting the rest of Dupin's fine work to colorless newspaper reporters. Dupin waved away my assertion, revealing with considerable pride that his young friend and chronicler had been the temperamental and brilliant poet Charles Baudelaire. I was impressed. Further, I found enticing Dupin's revelation that Baudelaire actually had written more than a hundred heretofore unknown accounts of his friend's investigations, none of which held up to the poet's own obsessive standards for publication, but all of which were secretly archived at Le Rossignol. Dupin then crossed into discourtesy by asserting that even the worst of Baudelaire's accounts was far better written than any penned by my "little military friend, Watson." I attempted to defend Watson's writing but was quickly reminded of the uselessness in opposing the egotism of any genuinely brilliant Frenchman. Still, don't misunderstand. I was honored by his presence. He was both as brilliant and as decadent as depicted, and our conversation that day in my rooms could be the stuff of a fine West End production. What matters here, however, is that Dupin offered me access to the secret, unpublished accounts of all his cases, even those that had resulted in failure. He had established a trust, for perpetuity, to attend to taxes and general upkeep of the shop, which was never open for business. Further, he explained that, in the more than two decades since the early death of Baudelaire, he had met no one deserving of his spiritual legacy, which, despite his reservations about what he described as my perverse combination of "overblown public fame and absurd personal monasticism," he bestowed upon me.

He was dead of a malignant tumor a few months later.

In the years since, I had accessed Le Rossignol on a few occasions; none, however, since the end of the Great War.

"This shop could use a good dusting and a bit of airing out," Mrs. Watson observed as we entered, closing the door behind us.

The air was stale but not fetid.

Whoever served as caretaker of the shop, doubtless unaware of the secrets it contained, took admirable precaution against vermin penetrating the premises. The place was as effectively sealed as an Egyptian tomb.

"What, exactly, are we looking for?" Mrs. Watson asked.

About then, I experienced a strange moment of disquiet, as I had never before felt in this place. Nor anywhere else. It was not danger but was ill-defined and disturbing nonetheless. A chill. Not of death. Worse. Of passing. Of obscurity. Worse yet, of negation.

I looked around. Nothing had changed here since my last visit.

So I let the sensation go.

"If this shop contains so many secrets," Mrs. Watson asked as we moved through the freshly stirred motes toward a large set of bookshelves labeled True Crime, "then why did Dupin make access so simple that literally any key would open the door? Is there a secret passageway or secret panel, or some other impediment in here?"

I shook my head.

"A safe?" she continued.

"No safe." I removed a small electric torch from my jacket pocket and shined the light on a bookshelf. "You can see that all the books are alphabetized by author. Quite conventional." When I got to the Bs I heard her gasp.

Baudelaire, *The Mystery of M. Paget*.
Baudelaire, *The Murders in the Musée d l'Orangerie*.
Baudelaire, *The Sacrificial Lynx*.

And so on . . . Two entire shelves of bound, handwritten manu-scripts, each an edition of one.

Mrs. Watson continued, incredulously, "So, there's no guard, no real lock on the front door, no safe inside, and no attempt to hide these treasures whatsoever, even to the point of categorizing and alphabet-izing them to make access easier?"

I moved my light across the shelves, looking for a particular title.

"What kind of madness is this?" she inquired.

I turned to her. "Have you read 'The Purloined Letter', one of the three authorized accounts of Dupin's cases?"

"Yes, it's quite famous."

I said nothing, allowing her to come to the conclusion herself.

After a moment, her face brightened. "Of course!" she said. She summarized aloud the pertinent elements of the story, perhaps to better jog her memory, "The police know with certainty that a stolen letter of incalculable value is hidden in a particular room, but for all their efforts they can't find it. Not in the vents or the plumbing, inside the furniture or behind framed pictures. Is that the one, Sherlock?"

I nodded.

She continued. "But when Dupin is called in to consult, he finds the letter almost immediately. How? By looking for it right out in the open. The least likely place of concealment . . . that is, hidden in plain sight."

"Yes, and that is the self-referential premise for Dupin's own hidden depository."

"Ingenious," she muttered.

I came at last to the title I'd been seeking: Baudelaire, *The Death of E. A. Poe*.

With the manuscript in hand, I led her from the book shop, "locking" the door after us. I doubt it has been opened since, except by its anonymous caretaker. Mrs. Watson will likely never have reason to return. So, one day very soon, I will be obliged to choose a suitable keeper of Dupin's secret archive. Or perhaps I should leave it to fate, entrusting the knowledge to whoever finds this manuscript.

ॐ

Mrs. Watson and I exited the shadowy Rue des Saints-Péres and returned to the bustling, brightly lit Boulevard Saint-Germain, starting back in the direction of our hotel; however, we got only a few steps before she stopped me on the pavement, and asked, "Can't we just dip into one of these cafés, find a quiet corner, and have a look at *The Death of E. A. Poe* now? It's all so . . . exciting!"

Actually, I had planned on reading the material alone when we got back to the hotel. Whatever I discovered of pertinence in the text I'd relate to her later. But, now, I saw this would disappoint her.

Once, I wouldn't have allowed her hankering to dissuade me from my plan. But having so recently been accused of *fastidiousness* . . .

"Good idea, Mrs. Watson," I said at the Place Saint-Germain-des-Prés.

She smiled delightedly.

So we turned into the nearest café, *Le Deux Magots*. Though noisy and more crowded with money-slinging American expatriates than I'd have preferred, we found an open table in a darkened corner where I thought it unlikely we'd be disturbed; there, we settled beside one another, like a retired British couple on holiday, and ordered drinks, she a Dubonnet cocktail and I a brandy.

I opened the bound, handwritten manuscript.

Her aged, red-rimmed eyes brightened. My heart beat a little faster too.

Mrs. Watson read Baudelaire's pinched but elegant handwriting on the title page aloud.

I turned to page one.

Mrs. Watson's French was not as good as mine, so I translated aloud the account of the investigation of the death of E. A. Poe:

One morning at Paris, upon awakening from
a languorous slumber, I took my ablutions,
breakfasted lightly, and was enjoying what
had become my regular twofold luxury of
silent rumination and a meerschaum, with my
companion C. Auguste Dupin, in the disheveled library at our residence at No. 33
Rue Dunôt, Faubourg St. Germain. Curling
eddies of smoke oppressed the atmosphere of
the chamber when I glanced up from my book
to my friend. I could see from his posture
that a deep reverie was upon him. Possessed of analytical faculties far beyond
those of any man I have ever met, Dupin
was fond, almost to the point of obsession, with enigmas, conundrums, and hiero-
glyphics. Much as a muscled man exults
in physical ability, delighting in exer-
cises that call his strength into action,
so glories the analytical mind in whatever moral activity *disentangles* uncertainties. My friend's solutions to enigmas
often exhibited a degree of ingenuity that
appeared to ordinary understanding to be
supernatural. His results, which seemed to
be the result of this uncanny intuition,
were actually brought about by the very
soul and essence of method.

I stopped reading, turning to Mrs. Watson. "Dupin's chronicler
Baudelaire went on to do fine things as a poet, but, in these nonfiction
accounts, he lacked the facility of our John when it came to composing
compelling, popular prose."

She grinned. "Yes, John had a gift."

"Indeed."

"Nonetheless, read on," she requested.

I scanned through the next half dozen paragraphs, which elaborated upon the moody reveries that overcame Dupin during periods of investigative quiet. According to Baudelaire, Dupin responded to such periods not with the anxiety from which I suffered but with what seemed an altogether more Gallic response, "giving the Future to the winds, slumbering tranquilly in the Present, and weaving the dull world around him into dreams." However, having met Dupin myself, I suspect he and I were not so different in our *natural* responses to the absence of formidable mental exercise, despite Baudelaire's depiction. Rather, I believe our contrary responses to such lulls resulted from our respective choices of cure for what would otherwise be the same attendant melancholy. Quite famously, a solution of cocaine served as my remedy, whereas I suspect Dupin's choice tended more toward some variant of opiate. Regardless, Baudelaire's description of the dreamy silence that he and Dupin shared in the house at 33 Rue Dunôt, Faubourg St. Germain carried on far longer than Dr. Watson would ever condone, which illustrates the indulgence one may expect when having a genius poet as one's chronicler, so I skipped silently ahead in my perusal, turning pages until I came at last upon something of relevance to the narrative.

```
Just as we'd begun our luncheon, we were
interrupted by two callers, one of whom
occupied a position of such importance that
we could not keep the pair waiting in the
foyer until after we finished our fare, as
we'd have preferred. We set our napkins on
the table and made our way to meet them.
The first of the two awaiting us in the
parlor, which was comfortably provisioned
with decades' old furniture and was dimly
lit by candles, as we habitually shuttered
our windows during the day to repel the
garish sun, was our acquaintance, Monsieur
G——, the Prefect of the Parisian Police.
Had he called alone, we'd have made him
```

wait until we finished our fare. However,
the second caller was of true interest,
being a gentleman of whom we had heard
but had not previously met. He introduced
himself, Monsieur R——, ambassador to France
from the United States of America. He complimented Dupin on the unusual green shade
of his eyeglasses, though this may have
been a politician's mere crafty concealment
of what was more likely a conservative disapproval and depreciation of the unusual.
Whichever, we gave the ambassador a hearty
welcome, offering an afternoon aperitif,
which he declined in the disappointingly
American fashion of claiming never to drink
before this or that hour of the day.

The barmaid interrupted us to ask if Mrs. Watson and I required
second drinks. Considering the sentence we had just read in the
manuscript about declining drinks, we both opted not to disappoint,
so we acceded to more liquor. Small sacrifice indeed.

"But when will we get to Poe?" Mrs. Watson asked.

I scanned the next few pages, wherein Dupin is engaged on behalf
of the United States government to travel to Washington, DC, to
investigate a suspected plot to assassinate the recently elected American
president, Zachary Taylor, thereby placing the narrative firmly in 1849,
despite Baudelaire's proclivity to refer to all such dates as 18—. After
enduring a difficult Atlantic crossing, the two Frenchmen arrive in the
American capital. In a private meeting at the White House, the interior
of which Baudelaire compares unflatteringly to numerous palaces he
has visited east of Suez, President Taylor explains to his French guests
why he believes someone is attempting to poison him. At this point,
however, Baudelaire interrupts the story of political assassination on
the grounds that he has chronicled the case elsewhere, presumably in
another volume now filed in Le Rossignol, and turns his attention to an

unexpected knock that came later that night on their hotel room door in Washington, DC. The visitor is the distinguished American essayist, critic, and short story writer Edgar Allan Poe, who has not made the forty-mile journey from Baltimore in hopes of conducting an interview for publication with the famous Dupin, as Baudelaire initially surmises, but, rather, because he is desperate to secure the brilliant Dupin's investigative assistance for himself. Poe too, it seems, is being stalked by an assassin. Because Dupin, an avid reader in many languages, is an admirer of Poe's horror stories and poems, particularly "The Raven," he agrees to hear out the frantic gentleman.

"We come to Poe at last," Mrs. Watson said, sipping from her Dubonnet cocktail.

However, we were just then interrupted at our corner table by a handsome American with a moustache and a boxer's musculature. I recognized him from the author photograph on the back of his celebrated novel *Fiesta*, which was still a subject of conversation among the undergraduates at Cambridge. The book had been published to even greater success in the United States, with the more ecclesiastical title *The Sun Also Rises*. The young man's name was Ernest Hemingway, and, unfortunately, it seemed he had recognized me too.

"Mr. Holmes," he said, thankfully taking care that no one overheard.

There was no point in denying my identity, as I hadn't taken the precaution of a disguise. "Mr. Hemingway," I answered.

He looked surprised and then gratified that I'd recognized him. He turned to Mrs. Watson and extended his hand. Clearly, he'd been drinking; nonetheless, his manner was respectful. "Please call me Ernest," he said to her.

"This is Mrs. Watson," I said, before she could offer him the informality of her first name.

They shook.

"*That* Watson?" he asked her.

"Yes, John was my husband."

"My condolences," he said. Then he pulled a third chair to our small table and turned to me. "May I sit?"

I looked around the room. Many heads already had turned our way. "Well, as you're hovering above us seems to draw more attention than would your sitting, I suppose it's the better alternative, for the moment at least," I said, closing Baudelaire's manuscript, as the last thing I wanted was to share its contents with, of all things, an ambitious young author.

"I didn't mean to draw any attention to you, Mr. Holmes," Hemingway said. "My apologies. I understand that you wouldn't want the entire café hounding you for autographs."

"That's kind of you to acknowledge, but I believe in this neighborhood yours is now the more famous face."

"Only because your face has gained the 'transmogrifying grace of age.'" He spoke the phrase as if complimenting me.

"I don't know the source of that quote," I said.

"Ovid," he answered.

He was making it up. I knew Ovid backward and forward and *The Metamorphosis* contained no such phrase, even taking into account an unconventional translation. This Hemingway was a formidable one.

"When I saw you across the room, I knew I'd never forgive myself if I did not take a moment to express my admiration for your work," he offered.

I nodded.

He continued, seeming, like many drinkers, to speak his words as he thought them. "I believe that the profession of detective on the darkened paths of crime may be the nearest thing to that of the soldier in war. Except . . ." He stopped, rethinking his words. "Well, maybe there's nothing that actually comes close to soldiering."

"I'm sure you're right, young man," I acknowledged. I had never been to war. I suspected Hemingway knew that. Was he taunting me? I didn't care. I'd allow him that, seeing as his book jacket biography identified him as a wounded veteran. And I knew what war did to men. I'd seen what it had done to John, who often woke up at night screaming. When I'd race into his room, I'd find him sitting up, drenched in sweat, but remembering nothing of the nightmare. And I suspect that Hemingway's mechanized war of trenches, the Somme, Verdun, the

Marne, Gallipoli, sixteen million dead, was of a darker nature than even what John had endured in Afghanistan.

"Perhaps it's more accurate to suggest that the work of the detective is the nearest to that of the writer and vice versa," he continued. "I refer to the continual pushing forward, clue by clue or page by page, with no guarantee of success and the genuine possibility, at any moment, of self-destruction."

"I wouldn't know about writing," I said. "My friend John Watson pursued the page for my benefit. But I'll take your word for the comparison, Mr. Hemingway. You seem quite fit to make it."

"Ah, you think me foolish, Mr. Holmes," the younger man said, looking genuinely admonished.

I did not think him altogether foolish. "I suspect you are most formidable."

An uncomfortable silence was broken only when Mrs. Watson asked, "Do you enjoy living in Paris, Mr. Hemingway?"

"Yes, but my wife and I are leaving soon," he said. "Back to the States."

"You've grown tired of your apartment on Rue Férou?" I asked.

Hemingway looked at me with an expression I'd seen often before. Wonder and vague discomfort. "How did you know where I lived, Mr. Holmes?"

I shrugged. "A guess. But not uninformed."

"Please, go on."

I always made *them* ask for the explanation. Unwelcome pedantry was a quality I sought to avoid. "When you stood at our table I observed three pamphlets in your jacket pocket, informally fanned like playing cards. Being both a fastidious and somewhat vain man, you'd surely not leave such handouts in your clothing any longer than necessary, suggesting you have collected them in just the past hours, presumably since leaving your residence. I took particular note of their order. Taken in reverse, they trace your movements these past few hours. I observed on top a schedule for upcoming productions at the *Théâtre du Vieux-Colombier*, located just a few streets from here. Are you planning to attend the *Comédie-Francaise* before you and your wife leave Paris?" I didn't wait for an answer. "And beneath that schedule is the printed bulletin from *Saint-Sulpice*, where a mass is held every Saturday evening at six o'clock." I looked at my watch. "Yes, just a few hours ago. Now, you may not be Catholic yourself, Mr. Hemingway, but perhaps your wife?" Again, I allowed no time for an answer. "The church, then, was your second stop after leaving your residence. And, finally, beneath the two documents in your pocket, thereby collected first on your leisurely walk here, is a brochure of upcoming books from the publisher, *Editions Athos*, located on the corner of the residential Rue Férou and the commercial Rue de Vaugirard, directly across from the Luxembourg Gardens. *Editions Athos* is named for the character from *The Three Musketeers*, who, in the novel, lived on Rue Férou. Now, might that detail appeal to a literary man seeking an apartment?" Once more, I continued without allowing even a breath for him to answer my question. "Of course you might have come to that street corner from some place in Montparnasse, but if you had, considering the light rain this afternoon, your shoes would show signs of mud from crossing the Luxembourg Gardens. Bearing no such mud leads me to presume you merely walked down your own street to the corner, collected the catalogue, and then doubled back in this direction, stopping at the church, the theater, and, finally, this table. Of course, I could be wrong."

"How do you know I didn't walk *around* the Luxembourg Gardens to reach that street corner?" he inquired.

"Because you're not the kind of man to walk 'around' anything."

He looked pleased with the characterization. "And how do you know I didn't approach that corner from the east or the west, Mr. Holmes?"

"Because Rue de Vaugirard is closed on the north side of the street for sewer repairs. Mrs. Watson and I happened by there earlier today on our cab ride from the train station to our hotel. Of course, you could have stepped your way through the construction, but that would have left a different tell-tale coating of mud on your shoes."

"You keep a map of Paris in your head?"

"I find it useful to keep 'maps' of numerous capitals in my head."

He looked down at the table, tapping it with his knuckles. "Well, damn. I do live on Rue Férou."

"Yes, but what does it really matter?" I asked.

"True, considering that we're leaving Paris."

"Actually, I meant it in consideration of your leaving our table, Mr. Hemingway. Most respectfully . . . But Mrs. Watson and I *are* occupied."

"Oh, my apologies," he said, standing. Only then did he glance at the manuscript we'd taken from Le Rossignol, which bore its title on its spine.

I glanced at the document. "A mere trifle."

"Poe was no trifle," Hemingway said.

"Agreed."

He leaned over us, setting his hands on our table, and addressed us with a certainty that went beyond the professorial. I suspected such confidence would make him even more famous in the years to come. And doomed. "Of course," he said, "for all Poe's influence, he is not an essential part of *authentic* American literature. He remained too fixated, stylistically, with England and the Continent. Real American writing didn't begin until Twain."

I looked up at him. "I think you're being insincere, Mr. Hemingway. Falsely modest. It will never suit you. The truth is you don't actually consider your country's literature as having begun until now, with *you*. Isn't that so?"

He smiled as he straightened.

"Good luck with that, Mr. Hemingway," I said.

He nodded a gracious farewell to Mrs. Watson and passed back into the crowded café.

"Quite the preening peacock," Mrs. Watson observed.

I tossed some franc notes onto the table and stood. "Now that my cover is blown, whatever Hemingway's intentions to keep it to himself, I think it best that you and I finish reading Mr. Poe's misadventure back at our hotel."

"But there's no lobby or lounge there."

I grinned. "This is Paris, Mrs. Watson. No one will turn his head if you come to my room."

She blushed, but assented.

It was there that we'd finish Baudelaire's account.

CHAPTER EIGHT

Monsieur Poe was distraught, his ordinarily pale complexion seeming to further whiten before our eyes as he related details of the recent attack upon his residence in Baltimore. Ill at ease in our hotel room, his anxiety remained undampened despite Dupin's fortifying him with a glass of good Armagnac, which we'd transported across the Atlantic in a rosewood box. Poe drank the Armagnac in a single draught, without seeming to savor or even to take note of its exceptional quality. We might as well have given him a shot of the local Virginia concoction, referred to as "White Lightning," which, while quite strong, is better used, I suspect, as liniment for rubbing down horses than for human consumption. Accordingly, Dupin did not offer him a second glass of the Armagnac, but chose instead to attempt to calm the nearly hysterical man with well-chosen words.

"Start at the beginning, Monsieur Poe," Dupin requested, a paragon of reassuring calm.

Poe nodded, signifying not only his assent but also, perhaps, attempting to clear his brain. "My apartment was in wild disorder," he said. "The furniture was broken and thrown in all directions. On my desk lay my own razor, besmeared with blood. On the hearth were three strands of grey fur, also dabbled in blood, seeming to have been pulled out by the roots. I recognized the shade of the fur. It had come from my own cat, which had not greeted me as she usually did upon my arrival and was nowhere to be seen. The innocent beast deserved no such violence. Moments later, I discovered its corpse tossed atop the armoire. At this, my horror, trepidation, and grief trebled."

Poe stopped to compose himself.

"Were any articles removed from the room?" Dupin asked.

Poe shook his head. "The armoire, like the chest of drawers, had been opened and rifled, although many articles still remained inside and, when my terrible accounting was complete, it was only my poor pet that had been taken from me, ruling out robbery and suggestive of something far, far worse!"

I lay on my back, stretched out on the hotel bed, the manuscript held before me like any ordinary nighttime reading. Meanwhile, Mrs. Watson sat in the near corner of my room, upright on a hard chair that allowed for no other posture. She looked quite uncomfortable, though she'd insisted on the arrangement. I'd offered to take the chair. But she considered it unseemly to sit on a man's bed, even when the man in question did not also occupy it, even under platonic circumstances such as ours.

"Shall I go on, Mrs. Watson?"

She looked at me as if I were mad. "Why wouldn't you, Sherlock?"

There was a slight slur to her words. Two Dubonnet cocktails were more alcoholic drink than she usually allowed herself.

"There are further descriptions of violent acts here," I explained. "Perhaps it would be better for me to scan through the manuscript myself and then review it for you afterward."

She waved away the idea, her speech loosened from its usual tenor. "I was married to John, who, need I remind you, wrote plenty about violence. He wrote about you, for Heaven's sake. And I lived in the same building as the two of you for all those years, with the comings and goings, up and down my stairs, of the *most disreputable ruffians in the city*. And in those years they came to know me by name. And I them! So please don't think of me as a fragile flower, Sherlock."

"My apologies," I said.

She closed her eyes. "Now, read on."

I turned back to the manuscript, glancing down the page, skipping a paragraph that recorded Poe's description of the particular horrors committed upon his cat, before I began to read aloud again:

```
"Do you think the actions of your assail-
ants, in regards to your unfortunate pet,
were intended as a reference to your famous
short story, 'The Black Cat'?" Dupin asked
Poe.
    "No, their violence far exceeded even
that story," Poe answered. "They intended
it as a warning to me."
    "How can you be sure?" Dupin inquired
    "The note."
    "Tell me about this note the assail-
ants left behind," Dupin requested of the
author.
    "Better yet, I've brought the note with
me," Poe replied.
```

I was interrupted in my reading of Baudelaire's account by the sound of gentle snoring. Mrs. Watson had fallen asleep, still sitting up in the wooden chair. I don't know how many hours of slumber she had

managed the previous night, her head resting on her arms on a table in
the reading room of the British Library. Nor can I say whether or not
she had napped on the Channel crossing as had I. For a woman in her
late seventies, it had been a taxing day. Nonetheless, I suspected the
two drinks at Le Deux Magots, rather than the day's frenzied pace, had
done her in.

I set the manuscript aside, stood up from the bed, and went to her.

"Mrs. Watson?" I whispered.

The only movement was a fluttering behind her eyes, as if she were
dreaming.

"Mrs. Watson?" I repeated, this time in full voice and placing my
hand softly on her shoulder.

Nothing. She was out cold.

I considered my options. Leaving her in the chair for the night
would doubtless result in aches and pains that she could ill afford come
morning, particularly if she also awoke with a "hangover." Could I carry
her out of my room and down the hall to her own? No. She was quite
light, but then so was I, relative to what I had once been. And calling
downstairs for assistance getting her to her room was out of the question, as it would mortify her to learn in the morning that not only her
drunkenness but also her presence in my room had been revealed to
a stranger, even if the stranger was a Parisian hotel night clerk. Fortunately, I was still strong enough to get her to my bed, which I did
by placing my hands under her arms and hauling her limp frame up
from the chair; no easy task. I then drew her close, as if in embrace,
and pivoted in a series of awkward dance steps to the mattress, where,
taking a deep and fortifying breath, I laid her as gently as possible, her
head upon one of the two pillows. She did not stir during the process.
While I had not pulled down the sheets and covers, I nonetheless took
a blanket from the end of the bed and placed it over her.

I could have taken her room key from her handbag and proceeded
down the hall to sleep in her bed.

But I didn't.

Why should I leave my own room? Besides, wouldn't it confuse her to awake alone in the morning here? Such a bewilderment would carry further weight because our investigation included the threat of violence. So, I retrieved the manuscript from the empty side of the bed and went to the wooden chair. Unfortunately, it was as uncomfortable as I'd suspected. However, that same discomfort likely aided me in remaining awake long enough to finish Baudelaire's manuscript, which included details of the murder of Edgar Allan Poe.

I would have much to relate to Mrs. Watson come morning.

Then, sometime in the night, I dropped the manuscript to the floor and fell asleep in the chair.

To my wonderment, I awoke elsewhere.

I noticed the purple light of morning through my hotel room window.

I was lying on the bedspread, fully dressed, beside Mrs. Watson. I had no recollection of moving from the chair to the bed. Surely, she had not awakened and carried me. So, I must have switched off the light and stumbled there half-asleep. My first thought was to get up. But then I noticed that Mrs. Watson, who lay on her side facing me, had opened her eyes.

"You can stay as you are," she said.

The slur was gone from her speech, and I knew she was no longer impaired.

So I relaxed back into my pillow.

"The sun's not even up yet, Sherlock. So let's sleep a little longer, all right?"

"Yes," I said.

She closed her eyes.

I closed mine, too, and in no time drifted back to sleep.

It was after eight when Mrs. Watson's sitting up on the bed awoke me.

I turned to her, hoping she'd not be offended by our impropriety.

I needn't have worried.

She smiled as she set the blanket aside and stood up, stretching her neck and shoulders. "I have to get back to my room to put myself together," she said. "I'm sure you have a very active day planned for us. Did you finish reading the manuscript?"

I nodded.

"You can tell me about it downstairs at breakfast."

"Yes."

She picked up her purse and searched out her room key. She turned back to me. "Good morning, Sherlock."

"Good morning, my dear."

She tapped the end of the bed twice with her fingertips, a punctuation of sorts, and then left my room.

I fell back onto my side of the bed, looking up at the ceiling. There was much to do today, though what I'd read in Baudelaire's account made me uncertain as to the next move. Perhaps reviewing the account with Mrs. Watson would stir an analytical breakthrough, I hoped.

And then, briefly, I stopped thinking about the case altogether.

At seventy-three years old, I had never before spent an entire night in bed with another person.

How strange and wonderful that it had been John's widow.

❦

Downstairs in the hotel's tiny breakfast room, Mrs. Watson and I shared tea and pastries as I related to her the substance of Baudelaire's report.

"The note left in Poe's disheveled room revealed the assailants' demands," I said. "They objected to assertions in the author's recently published essay, 'Eureka,' and warned him against referring to particular sections of the work in the lecture tour he was scheduled to undertake."

"And the part of the essay to which they objected?"

"You can likely guess, Mrs. Watson."

"The part about multiple worlds," she surmised, accurately.

I quoted from Poe's essay: "'. . . a limitless succession of Universes, more or less similar to that of which we have cognizance.'"

"What happened then?"

"Dupin undertook an exhaustive investigation, beginning with a visit to the New York offices of the essay's beleaguered publisher, and, after a series of bold maneuvers, concluding with a consultation in the crypt beneath St. John the Evangelist Church in Manhattan, Dupin uncovered a conspiracy involving a powerful cabal opposed to any public promotion of what Baudelaire labels *univers parallèles*."

"And this cabal was the Eureka Society?" she asked.

I nodded. "In Baudelaire's account, the assassination plot is referred to as the 'Eureka Project,' though I suspect the conspirators currently threating Conan Doyle are ideologically descended from this earlier incarnation, with significant variations to account for our modern era."

"Why couldn't Poe just cancel his lecture tour, if his life was threatened?" she asked.

"First, to do so would be against Poe's nature. The manuscript makes clear that the American was prideful to the point of self-destruction. But that's not all. There is a perverse, ironic turn as well. When the conspirators learned that Poe had secured the aid of the famous C. Auguste Dupin, whose *ratiocination* they respected, they adjudged that merely warning Poe was insufficient, concluding that the author, now aided by a personage of such renown, posed a greater risk than before and, consequently, had to be killed."

"So what did Dupin do?"

"He and Baudelaire raced back to Baltimore, finding Poe in his rooms. There, they explained to the troubled author that he'd been marked for death and that his only hope was to 'disappear.' However, a glance out the third story window indicated that even at that moment, just outside the flat, there hovered a pair of burly men who'd likely been employed to kill Poe. Dupin remained unfazed, entreating Baudelaire and his client to switch clothing. As Baudelaire was slightly larger than Poe, the American looked bedraggled in the new clothes, which, nonetheless, and more importantly, were quite different from the American author's signature black attire. The young Baudelaire's clothing was flamboyant and colorful and, thereby, potentially deceptive. His hat was particularly unique, being the sort only a French poet, or perhaps a musketeer, would dare to wear. 'Leave your documents of identification hidden here under the mattress and go straight to the train station, Mr. Poe,' Dupin beseeched. Poe agreed, expressing his gratitude."

I took a sip of tea.

"And?" Mrs. Watson pressed.

"Dupin and Baudelaire watched from the darkened window as Poe, in the big hat and ill-fitting clothing, exited the building, crossed the street, and safely maneuvered past the assassins. Indeed, a few minutes later, the two killers burst into Poe's room with clubs raised, only to find Dupin and Baudelaire sipping brandy and sharing passages from the Bible. Confused, the henchmen went away."

"So Poe disappeared?" Mrs. Watson asked. She didn't wait for an answer. "I thought he died under 'mysterious circumstances.'"

"Indeed, Baudelaire's chronicle lacks a felicitous ending," I answered. "Poe did *not* go straight to the train station, as instructed. Instead, he stopped at a public house for a 'constitutional.' Then another and another. There, apparently, the assassins discovered him, as the next morning he was found unconscious, brutally beaten while in 'someone else's clothing,' thereby creating a mystery about which newspapers speculated until Poe died in hospital a few days later, having never regained consciousness. In cruel obituaries, he was discredited as a crank, and his final essay 'Eureka' was ridiculed and soon forgotten. And there you have it."

"So, Dupin and Baudelaire returned to France?"

"Post haste," I said. "Aiding Poe, they too had crossed the conspirators. Indeed, Baudelaire admits at the end of his manuscript that he'd like to publish it, counting the adventure among his favorites, were it not that to do so would bring down the wrath of the cabal."

"Who is this cabal, Sherlock? Did the manuscript say? Is it the Church?"

I picked up my tea cup. "How do you reason that, Mrs. Watson?"

She shrugged. "Well, as you mentioned, the Church has long objected to any concept of *univers parallèles*. And why wouldn't they? After all, where would God fit into a multitude of universes?"

"That's an astute observation," I said.

"Thank you, Sherlock."

I considered my many years in Baker Street and the countless times I'd noted minute details of visiting strangers without ever truly having observed Mrs. Hudson. Now, I realized she might have assisted John and me on numerous investigations. But I'd failed *to observe*, the trait for which I am most celebrated. And failing to recruit her for assistance in our cases may have been the least of it. How many simple, companionable moments had I missed with her in those years? "Go on, Mrs. Watson. Your analysis is astute."

She hardly needed encouragement. "Well, if there existed countless versions of all of us, wouldn't we each be every manner of sinner, saint, and everything in between? In one universe or another, I mean. And, if that were so, then God's judgment of our souls would be impossible. Heaven and hell? All of it, threatened. And with that, the ultimate power of the Church."

"That's sound reasoning," I said. "A bit medieval, but sound."

She picked up her orange juice. "I'm glad it's sound, but is it correct?"

I nodded. "Church interests were indeed central to the Eureka Project in 1849. However, while the Church may still be peripherally involved, they cannot be the primary movers behind today's Eureka Society."

"Why not?"

"Because the Church no longer possesses the power to do so, however many inane conspiracy theories might be found daily in the *News of the World*. No, the Church has been humbled since the days of our unfortunate Mr. Poe."

"Humbled by what?"

I put down my tea. "By science, which insists on empirical evidence."

"Science existed in Poe's day," she observed.

"Yes, but not in the manner of today. Oh, 1849 was not 1549. Poe was not burned at the stake. But, remember, in the mid-nineteenth century Pius IX still exerted real power. As the last pope to reign over the Papal States, he decreed his own infallibility and struck hard against modernity. Since Poe's death, however, we've had Darwin, Faraday, Maxwell, Einstein, and the others. As a result, the Church no longer wields the power it did in Poe's day."

"So who wields such power?"

"Governments, international business, banks, organized crime, and various underground combinations thereof." Again, I thought fruitlessly of Moriarty.

"Then which among them . . . ?" she started.

"None, as matters currently stand," I interrupted.

Her face registered her surprise. "None? Why not?"

"The same answer," I said. "Science."

She shook her head, confused.

"As I said, ours is an age of empirical evidence. Mere irreligious, philosophical propositions, such as Poe's 'Eureka' or Conan Doyle's recent essay, no longer pose the same threats they once did to the powers that be."

"Yet Conan Doyle was shot."

"Indeed."

"So where does that leave us? I don't understand."

Nor did I.

After all, no entity powerful enough to accomplish the actions of the past weeks, beginning with the assassination attempt on Conan Doyle and continuing through the seemingly unnoticed dismantling of the Society for Psychic Research and the compromise of both police reports and newspaper coverage regarding my shooting of the blond assassin, would feel threatened by the mere anecdotal writings of Conan Doyle, a man whose greatest notoriety came as a scribbler of historical romances and speculative fiction. Our living prime minister's spectral, alternative appearance? Absurd. Yet the murderous intent with which the current incarnation of the Eureka Society had responded to news of such an appearance belied the absurdity. Multiple worlds? Nonsensical! It may be true, as Hamlet said to Horatio, that there are more things in Heaven and Earth than are dreamt of in our philosophy. But of what use today is such a vague recognition of the Unknowable absent hard evidence? What possible threat to true power can any such unsupportable concept pose?

Thus, my thoughts spiraled.

Mrs. Watson took a deep breath, sorting it through. "So, today's Church lacks the power, while the institutions that possess such power lack the motivation. Is that how you see it, Sherlock?"

"Something close to that," I acknowledged. A conundrum. Or perhaps just a dead end.

"So what are we to do next?"

I hadn't a good answer to Mrs. Watson's question. Nor to the essential question she hadn't asked: what was the source behind Conan Doyle's identifying me in Cambridge in the first place? Absent answers, I dissembled. "This is not the most private place to discuss such matters," I observed, glancing around the deserted breakfast room.

She turned toward the kitchen. "Oh, I don't think Madame even speaks English," she countered.

"You don't *think* she does?" I said. "Meaning you're not certain."

"Ah," she answered, catching my conspiratorial tone. She lowered her voice to a whisper. "Yes, we'll talk later."

I looked at my watch. "Let's finish breakfast, Mrs. Watson. We'll stop at Le Rossignol to return the manuscript and then make our way onto to the next ferry train for London."

"And then?" she queried.

I merely smiled.

After a moment, she nodded slyly, as if my confident expression was all the answer she needed.

Of course, I'd offered her no real answer to her question.

What was my plan?

At that moment, I planned simply to return to London, assume a new disguise, and divide my time surveilling the offices of the counterfeit Society for Psychic Research and the regular residence of Conan Doyle. Unobtrusive observation. Nothing brilliant. Ordinary detective work. In other words, starting over. But I never put that modest agenda into effect. Rather, upon our return to my Bloomsbury safe house late that same night, we would discover circumstances altered such that no further surveillance was required. Matters of immediate urgency would impel our attentions. Of course, as Mrs. Watson and I stood from the table in the breakfast room of the Hotel de la Sorbonne, I did not yet know what dramatic turns awaited us.

"One last question before we leave," she said, setting her napkin down beside the empty basket of pastries.

"Yes?"

She pointed to my plate. "Are you going to finish that croissant, Sherlock?"

"No, my dear. Please, take it."

In some other world did I answer differently?

CHAPTER NINE

"So you're saying that now you believe in séances?" Conan Doyle asked me late that night, shortly after Mrs. Watson and I arrived in Bloomsbury, both of us weary from the day's travel and perhaps slightly unprepared for the scribbler's spirited response to the brief summation I'd offered him of the investigation's previous seventy-two hours.

"If you mean by séances a systematic manner of contact between this world and a 'world of the dead,' conducted by a professional medium, then no," I answered, seated at one end of the sofa in the front parlor, "I don't believe in séances."

Mrs. Watson sat at the other end of the sofa, quietly taking it in.

Coming from the train station, I'd offered to drop her at her house on Belgrave Square. But as she already carried her overnight bag, with her cosmetics and a second change of clothes, she had opted to join me here. This house had plenty of bedrooms. I suspect she wanted to participate in Conan Doyle's debriefing, as the case had captured her imagination.

Meanwhile, Conan Doyle paced the room before us. Though it was almost midnight, he showed no fatigue, exhibiting a physical vigor enviable for any man of his age. Doubtless, his enforced, solitary confinement, regardless of the residence's comfortable furnishings and well-stocked kitchen, had served to intensify not only his restlessness but also his natural gregariousness.

"But didn't you just say you thought the manifestation of this spirit version of Prime Minister Baldwin, or, rather, the non-Prime Minister Baldwin, might indeed have been real?" he pressed me, gesturing with his arms like a barrister attempting to make a point before the bench.

I sighed, but then reminded myself that Conan Doyle's questions were not unreasonable or insignificant, particularly as it was he who'd been shot. "What I actually just said, Sir Arthur, was that I did not believe Madame Du Lac created a fraudulent 'spirit' in the home of Lady Vale Owen."

"But if the spirit was not 'fraudulent,' then it must have been real," he responded.

"I did not say it was 'not fraudulent.'" The last thing I wanted was a semantic confrontation. But it seemed I had no choice. "I said only that Madame Du Lac did not create the illusion."

"Then who did?" he demanded. "And how?"

For this, I had no answers.

"And what of the *univers parallèles* that Poe wrote about?" he continued.

"It is scientifically unsupported, my dear Conan Doyle."

"Yes, but not so long ago the same could have been said of the wireless."

"The wireless is a technological development," I replied.

"True," he countered, "but the theory behind its development, invisible electromagnetic waves, would have seemed pure balderdash as recently as our own youths, Mr. Holmes!"

I shrugged in acknowledgement, somewhat surprised that Conan Doyle understood something as modern as the workings of a wireless. Nonetheless, I found his display of credulity unappealing. So I offered what I hoped would be sufficient to conclude the conversation. "Despite my unwavering rejection of Spiritualism," I said, "I am willing to acknowledge that I cannot as yet offer any conventional explanation for the manifestation you witnessed."

Conan Doyle made a fist, as if he had just scored the winning penalty kick in a football game. "Then you agree that *all is possible*."

"That's not what I said," I murmured, too weary to further argue the point.

He seemed not to have heard me. "The thesis of my latest essay, which I wrote yesterday at that desk," he said, pointing, "is that contact with invisible worlds is indeed possible."

"Fine," I answered dismissively, glad for whatever distraction writing an essay had provided him. It is not easy to be a house prisoner, particularly for a man as energetic as Conan Doyle.

"It would be a pleasure to read your new essay, Sir Arthur," Mrs. Watson said.

"I'd be most happy for your opinion, Mrs. Watson," he answered. "But I'm afraid I sent off the essay by this morning's post."

I turned, suddenly wide awake. "You did what?"

He shrugged. "Oh, I know some authors take more time with their work. But I did not earn my literary reputation for being 'prolific' by overthinking, overediting, or overwriting. I know what I want to write and I write it. Simple as that. I leave slaving over a manuscript to your neighbors here in Bloomsbury who take years to complete their novels. I wouldn't be interested in making their acquaintance even if I *were* free to walk out that door. They might be a bad influence on my work."

"I'm not concerned with your literary resourcefulness," I said, attempting to contain my anger and conceal my trepidation.

"You posted the essay from this house?" Mrs. Watson asked, following my line of reasoning.

He nodded. "Yesterday morning I saw a classified ad in the *Times* calling for essays regarding 'unusual experiences in the field of Spiritualism.' The pay is quite generous. So I got the essay right out to them. Naturally, I haven't heard back yet. But I thought it better to strike while the iron is hot."

"Turn off the lamp," I instructed Conan Doyle.

He looked at me oddly but did as I asked.

In the near darkness, I stood and went to the window, pulling back the drawn curtains just enough to peer out. "Well, you're right about the iron being hot," I said, turning back.

"What do you mean?" he asked.

"There are two large men standing in the shadows across the street. They're watching this house." Mrs. Watson and I had not noticed them upon our arrival, but I didn't doubt they'd been there. Nor that they'd noticed *us*.

"But how . . ." Conan Doyle stopped. He realized now the implications of his literary enthusiasm. "So the ad in the *Times* was a trap."

"Yes," I said.

"And I stepped into it," he continued.

"That's exactly the phrase that came to my mind, Sir Arthur," Mrs. Watson answered, somewhat earthily but not inaccurately.

"They must have witnessed our arrival, Mrs. Watson," I indicated.

"Yes, and we were undisguised. So they probably recognized you, Sherlock."

Very likely.

"Who are they?" Conan Doyle asked.

I turned to him. "I don't know."

"What will they do now?" he pressed.

"Judging from their previous actions," I said, "they'll wait a little longer to see if anyone else arrives and then burst into this house."

"And then?" he asked.

"You're the one with the bullet wound," I said to him. "Need I spell it out?"

"But who are they?" Conan Doyle repeated.

"I already said I didn't know," I snapped. "But perhaps if you walk outside, my dear Sir Arthur, you can share hearty handshakes all around while you politely ask for their calling cards."

"Don't be ridiculous, Holmes," he puffed.

Mrs. Watson stood up from the couch and made her way to the back of the house, peeking through a drawn blind. When she returned, her face was pale. "There are two more in the back as well."

"Turn the light back on," I instructed Conan Doyle. "We may delay them slightly by making them believe we're waiting for more associates to arrive."

"Are there more associates?"

"No."

"Are we armed?" Conan Doyle asked.

"No."

"Then let's call the police," Conan Doyle suggested.

I doubted the police would come to our aid, considering the scope of the conspiracy represented by the agents outside. But that was not the only problem. "Pick up the telephone receiver."

Conan Doyle did as I asked. He held it to his ear. "The line's dead."

"So what do we do now?" Mrs. Watson muttered.

I sat in a chair and removed my pipe from my jacket, calmly lighting it.

"What are you doing, Holmes?" Conan Doyle demanded. "We can't just be sitting ducks when they burst in!"

"What do you suggest, my dear sir? That we take defensive positions behind the sofa?"

"This is no time for sarcasm, Holmes," Conan Doyle objected.

I took a puff of my pipe.

"How dare you just sit there smoking?" Conan Doyle continued. "I am a man of action, and I insist upon the same manly, British attitude from you."

"Then why don't you demonstrate for me?" I suggested. "Why don't put up your fists, like Jack Dempsey, and walk outside. That would certainly qualify as 'action.'"

Mrs. Watson took a seat at my desk, watching. Her self-possession would have made John proud.

"How can you just sit there and smoke?" Conan Doyle repeated.

I answered. "As you may know from the celebrated writings of Mrs. Watson's dearly missed husband, I spent a few years away from the madding crowd, disappearing to foreign lands. One stop was in Japan. While at the Shunkōin Temple in Kyoto, I heard a story that might be instructive to you now."

"You're going to tell me a *story?*" he asked.

I didn't let his skepticism deter me. Or rush me. "One day, a young man was walking from one village to another when he was spotted at a distance by a hungry tiger who gave chase. The young man ran as fast as he could, but, naturally, the tiger gained ground, coming closer and closer. Just before the tiger made a meal of him, the young man arrived at a cliff with a sheer drop of more than a thousand feet. Industriously, he took hold of a vine and swung himself over the side just as the tiger arrived at the precipice. The tiger looked over the edge, slavering hungrily. Now dangling precariously, the young man noticed that a mouse had emerged from a hole in the cliff, near the top, and had begun gnawing at the vine, which thereby would break any moment, sending the young man down, down, down. Meanwhile, the tiger continued pacing patiently at the cliff's edge. That's when the young man noticed a wild strawberry growing on the cliff side just within his reach. He plucked it and ate. It was delicious."

Conan Doyle waited a moment before saying: "And? What happened next?"

"That's the end of the story."

He looked at me, quizzically.

I puffed on the pipe. "Delicious," I said.

"Ah," Conan Doyle murmured, comprehending. "So you're telling us we're goners?"

"Eventually, yes. Goners. It is the one certainty. But not tonight."

He brightened. "Then what's the plan?" he pressed. "That's what I've been asking for, not stories!"

Mrs. Watson smiled, as if she'd trusted I had a plan.

I pointed to the coat closet. "Hidden inside is a false floor and a passage that leads down to the city's vast sewer system." I removed the small electric lantern I'd carried since our journey the day before to Le Rossignol. "I know the sewers quite well. And I have a second safe house on Campbell Road in Islington, which we can reach without ever rising to the street. However, it will be a long and strenuous night. And, I must warn you, the neighborhood to which we'll arrive lacks the high-minded gentility of Bloomsbury. Indeed, it's the most crime ridden in London, which may serve our purposes by making it seem to others the last place we'd go for refuge."

"Then let's get out of here," he insisted.

I nodded and stood.

"What of our bags?" Mrs. Watson asked.

"I'm sorry Mrs. Watson, but we have to leave them behind, as we'll be pressing through some tight spaces in the sewers. My apologies also for any unpleasantness that will characterize our upcoming journey. For now, just take a moment to insure that your name appears nowhere on either your suitcase or any of its contents. The men outside may not have recognized you, as they likely recognized me."

"So, how will you show your face out of doors tomorrow?" she asked.

"As in this house, I keep in my Islington residence a closetful of clothing, wigs, prosthetics, stage make-up, and the like, for both men and women. So, don't worry. Tomorrow, we'll emerge with new faces as different, anonymous Londoners."

"Are we going to just stand here, enjoying strawberries until the vine breaks and we all fall to our deaths?" Conan Doyle asked.

I appreciated his apt and timely allusion. "No, it's time we went."

"Good," he said, starting for the hall closet.

Now, if I were Victor Hugo I'd provide numerous pages of description of our trek through the sewers. But I am not Hugo, so suffice to say that over the next few hours we coursed the unpleasant web of underground passages and made it to my second safe house just before sunrise.

Thus delivered, we wearily settled ourselves.

I don't know how much of the morning passed before I noticed an oversized envelope sitting atop a long-neglected pile of commercial fliers at the foot of the mail slot. Picking up the missive, I noted that its postmark indicated delivery just the day before. It was addressed to my fictional persona, Professor von Schimmel, recently of Cambridge University; the return address, Cambridge University physics department, indicated it was from Paul Dirac, the twenty-six-year-old physicist under whose office door I had slipped my Islington address before taking my recent, late-night leave of academia. I assumed the correspondence consisted of Dirac's latest paper on quantum mechanics, which I imagined I'd get to after I settled the urgent matters at hand. I looked forward to the casual distraction. I slit open the envelope, which, indeed, contained Dirac's latest paper. However, I did not set the pages aside, as planned. Rather, after I glimpsed the title, I immediately sat down to read the young physicist's work.

Many-Worlds:
A New Interpretation of the Wave Function
Collapse in Quantum Mechanics

Don't worry. I too was initially confused by the title.
But that "many worlds" business caught my attention.

❧

Within hours, Mrs. Watson and I had departed for Dirac's rooms in Cambridge.

We left Conan Doyle behind. I felt confident the scribbler would do nothing so foolish as to again post correspondence in our absence. The Islington residence, a ground-floor, cold-water flat, possessed no telephone, only intermittent electricity, and an ancient wood stove for heat. It was no Ritz suite. Naturally, Conan Doyle presented himself to me as a disgruntled prisoner when I told him he could not join us on the trip to Cambridge. I explained that traveling in pairs always draws less attention than as a trio; this would be particularly the case now, as the henchmen in Bloomsbury, who likely had burst into my house, discovered the secret passage, and, ultimately, lost our trail in the warren of sewers beneath the capital, would be looking above ground for a fleeing party of three. We could all three disguise ourselves, as Mrs. Watson and I did, but every trio moving through every train station would be subject to intense scrutiny from the conspirators. Or we could hire a car to take us all to Cambridge, but drivers sometimes worked as informers. Conan Doyle could not deny my logic and shook our hands with all good wishes when Mrs. Watson and I departed, late in the morning.

Leaving the safe house, Mrs. Watson and I looked little like ourselves.

She wore a long wig with a tiny hat pinned at an angle on her head, and make-up to create a sickly complexion, suggestive perhaps of a consumptive, or, at least, one with whom you might share your handkerchief but from whom you would never ask for it back. Serious illness is a great tool for keeping others at a distance.

Meantime, I returned to my disguise as professor of classical physics, Heinrich von Schimmel. This was, after all, how I'd been known to Dirac in Cambridge. In those hallowed halls, and elsewhere, my young colleague was considered a peer of the distinguished quantum theorists Niels Bohr and Werner Heisenberg, continentals who sought nothing less than a revolution in science equal to that of Einstein's a generation before. As Von Schimmel, I had enjoyed Dirac's vanguard explanations of the counterintuitive nature of the new science. In his latest paper, which I'd read at a pace in my grimy Islington safe house, he had given that counterintuitive quality its most dramatic twist to date.

Consequently, he was our man now.

But he did not answer his telephone when I rang him. Nonetheless, I considered it likely he would be available for consultation in his rooms that afternoon. He had no lectures that day and did not maintain a social schedule. So, absent appointment, Mrs. Watson and I made our way from Campbell Road to King's Cross Station, where I bought tickets on the 12:04 to Cambridge.

We settled into a compartment, which we had to ourselves, in the first-class carriage.

We'd be in Cambridge before tea time.

I recall the ride through the sunlit, green countryside as being quite refreshing after our dark and noxious journey through the sewers the night before and our morning's trek out of the squalid, coal-enshrouded environs of Campbell Road.

For a time, we rode in silence.

Mrs. Watson gazed out the window.

We were still someplace near Potter's Bar when she turned to me. "So, how does this Dirac fellow's work relate to the events of the past weeks? I mean, I've never seen you shuffling through typed pages with such breathless enthusiasm."

Characteristically, I'd offered only minimal explanation for our hurried departure. "Professor Dirac is a distinguished scientist," I said to her now, as if that were explanation enough.

It wasn't.

"What does his being a scientist have to do with Conan Doyle being shot and our being chased through the London sewers?" she asked.

I respected that she would not be put off. Also that she had developed a more pointed and, frankly, effective manner of questioning than our John had ever managed to put to me. "It's as I suggested in Paris," I answered. "If there were any scientific basis for the manifestation that Conan Doyle and my fraudulent mystic Siddhartha Singh publicly described, then such substantiation could explain why formidable, modern forces otherwise disinterested in the 'supernatural' have taken notice. Indeed, violent notice."

"And Dirac has proposed such a basis in his paper?"

I nodded.

"But how can that be?" she asked. "Science makes sense. This goes against all common sense."

"It does, and going against common sense is what this new science of quantum mechanics seems to be about. At least as I understand it. I am no expert. Hence, our journey to Cambridge."

"Well, I know nothing about 'quantum mechanics.' I never heard the term before."

"Then you'll have plenty to take in."

"I don't want to seem the imbecile, Sherlock."

"You could never seem less than highly intelligent, my dear."

"Can you at least tell me what 'quantum mechanics' is?"

A simple enough question. However, no quantum theorist has yet managed to fully answer it even in the latest scientific journals. I put it to Mrs. Watson as clearly as possible. "Quantum mechanics is the study of the way elementary particles, of which everything in the universe is made, including you, me, and the distant stars, behave."

"Behave? You make these particles sound like naughty schoolchildren."

"Actually, that image captures their character quite well."

"What do you mean?"

"Any change to a subatomic particle is perceptible only as a non-deterministic, physically discontinuous transition between discrete states . . ."

She stopped me. "What language are you speaking, Sherlock? I'm not following a word of it."

"Ah, forgive me for the overreliance on jargon." I reconsidered my approach to the explanation. "What I mean to say, Mrs. Watson, is that a subatomic particle . . ."

"Subatomic?" she interrupted.

"Smaller than an atom."

"That's small indeed," she said.

"A subatomic particle does not travel or evolve from one state to another, as we do," I continued, increasingly aware that quantum physics was not one of the disciplines in which I had achieved expertise in the years I'd masqueraded in various academic persona. But I was determined to be as clear as possible. "Rather, Mrs. Watson, such a particle simply 'becomes' something else, instantaneously. Accordingly, no particle can be observed in such a way as to identify both its current position and its angle of movement. We can only ever know where it is but not where it's going, or what direction it's been traveling but not where it is. The German scientist Werner Heisenberg calls this the 'uncertainty principle.' Or at least that's how I understand it." With this simple explanation, I had elevated Mrs. Watson's knowledge beyond that of most university physics professors, as Heisenberg's theory had been published just the year before in the journal *Zeitschrift für Physik* and had not yet been translated. Recommended to me by Dirac, I'd found it fascinating reading.

"So we can never know the whole story?" she said.

I thought her interpretation cut straight to the point. "That's right. What we're left with are mere statistical likelihoods that any particular particle will behave in a certain fashion, which, when applied to billions of particles as a whole, allows for very precise predictions indeed."

"But any one particle . . . unpredictable," she followed.

"Yes."

"Interesting," she observed. "But what does it have to do with our case, Sherlock?"

Good question. "This brings us to the apparent dualism of the 'wave' and 'particle' functions and how the Copenhagen Interpretation attempts to reconcile such a strange phenomenon."

She looked at me again as if I were speaking a foreign language.

I had to do better.

"In short," I continued, "when a particle is not observed it is actually more like a vast aggregation of possibilities than it is like a single entity, distinct and objective in place and time. Think of it as being like a hazy cloud of likelihoods that only congeals into a single, 'real' object when it is observed."

"Observed?" she queried.

"Measured."

"As by an instrument?"

"Yes, or . . . simply looked at."

"So *looking* at a subatomic particle makes it 'real'?" she muttered, not bothering to conceal her incredulity.

"I told you it would seem illogical, but it's all verifiable experimentally. This process of collapsing the wave function through the act of observation . . ."

"Wave function?"

"I mean, reducing the numerous possible states of a particle to a single 'real one,' via the act of observation. Quantum physicists call this 'the Copenhagen Interpretation.'"

She looked up at the train compartment's ceiling as she spoke, sorting it through. "So, the whole universe is made up of particles that only become 'real' when we look at them?"

"Something like that, Mrs. Watson."

She turned to me and narrowed her eyes. "Yet these odd particles are the building blocks of you, me, this train, the trees outside, the moon and the sun?"

"Yes."

"Ridiculous!" she said, sitting back in her chair and crossing her arms. "It's like some kind of music hall comedy routine. Absurd!"

I leaned toward her. "I don't disagree with you about that," I said. "Indeed, while standing in the queue back at Kings Cross, I conceived a thought experiment to illustrate that absurdity."

"Thought experiment?"

"An instructive scenario."

"I could use something like that."

I wasn't sure how useful she'd find my scenario. "Imagine that a dog is placed into a sealed metal box along with a radioactive particle, which, at a given moment, has a precisely 50 percent chance of decaying and releasing into the box a deadly gas. The moment comes and goes. However, since the box remains sealed, we, of course, cannot see inside to know the fate of the dog. It could be dead; it could be alive. All well and good so far, right?"

"No, it's not all right," Mrs. Watson pronounced. "It's pure animal cruelty. No dog deserves that!"

"It's just a thought experiment, my dear," I answered.

"No matter," she objected. "They're such faithful and loving creatures."

I thought of Toby, the good-natured dog who long ago had assisted Dr. Watson and me in one of our cases. And then I remembered Mrs. Watson's beloved terrier from years before. "Okay, let's make it a cat."

She sighed, as that was hardly better.

"In any case," I said, leaving animal cruelty for another discussion, "according to the currently accepted 'Copenhagen Interpretation,' until the box is actually opened, the animal inside remains literally both alive *and* dead. That is, only upon observation will it be *either* alive or dead."

"You mean only by observing can we know whether it is dead or alive," she surmised.

"That's also true. But it's not what I mean. Rather, only upon observation will the animal *become* either dead or alive. Until that moment, being unobserved, it is both alive and dead, simultaneously."

She shook her head. "To me, if an animal can be both alive and dead at the same time and it all just depends on whether we've looked to determine which is the case . . . Well, I'm sorry, but this 'Copenhagen Interpretation' is, as I said before, absurd."

I could not fault her. "But what if existence is precisely that?"

"What?" she asked.

"Absurd."

"Oh, now you're sounding like one of those continental philosophers, Sherlock."

That stung. But I'd been called worse. "Let me raise your ire even more with the alternative interpretation that forms the basis of Dirac's recent paper," I said.

"About this quantum business?"

I nodded. "Let's stay with the image of the animal in the box," I said. "What if the act of observation doesn't merely make the multiple possibilities congeal into a single, 'real world' event, but, instead, breaks the world into two, creating a kind of junction as on a branch. So, in one world the animal struts out of the box, alive, and in the other he's carried out, deceased. And both worlds are equally 'real,' each proceeding from that point forward ever independent of the other."

She looked at me. "*Univers parallèles.*"

"Yes, though, in our day-to-day existence, we never know that such divisions are continually occurring."

"And this new quantum interpretation from your friend Dirac proposes that such a thing is plausible in the modern world?"

I nodded.

She held the pad of her index finger to her lips and lowered her eyes, thinking. "Of course, you believe it's balderdash, right?"

"As I said to you before, what *I* believe is neither here nor there. What matters is what others believe and what that belief means to them."

"But even if it's so . . ." She stopped once more.

I waited. "Does this make sense to you?" I asked at last.

She answered without hesitation. "Not really."

"Then that means there's a chance I explained it properly, Mrs. Watson, as quantum mechanics makes sense to no one, including its brilliant progenitors, even if experiments indicate it is so."

"This is what we're going to discuss with young Dirac? His new theory of . . . what's he call it?"

"Many worlds."

"And this is 'science'?"

"It is a scientific proposition, grounded in advanced mathematics, experimental observation, and rational thought."

"Which makes it formidable in our modern world."

"Yes."

"And you're not playing some kind of game?" she asked. She did not wait for an answer. "I mean, reading John's accounts of your cases, one has a sense that you're always two or three moves ahead, just collecting confirmation and evidence of what you already know."

"It may be a game, but . . ." I shook my head. "In chess, one indeed plays three or four or more moves ahead. A good player may even know the outcome of a match as early as the opening exchange of pawns. But the chess board is limited to sixty-four squares. And, while the number of possibilities for any one move is vast, each choice is still bound by the board, whereas in the real world there are no such boundaries."

"Especially if there's more than one world," she said. She straightened her skirt and checked the pin on the strange little hat she wore on the side her head, as if pulling herself together from a taxing excursion. "Thank you for the tutorial, Sherlock. I won't feel like a complete fool when I meet this Professor Dirac. Even if this quantum business does leave one feeling rather like a woodland animal attempting to understand the design of an aeroplane."

"When you have eliminated the impossible, whatever remains, however improbable, must be the truth," I said, quoting John quoting me.

"Yes, I know," she answered. "I've read *The Sign of Four*." She turned back to the window, observing the passing countryside. "Look at all the wondrous things your chaotic little particles make."

I glanced outside.

I was never much for the beauty of nature for its own sake. But, in this instance, I nodded in agreement with Mrs. Watson's observation. Then I leaned back in my seat, closing my eyes. I was tired, having endured another sleep-deprived night, and I drifted off. The exhalation of air brakes, the hiss of steam, the grinding of metal, and the clanging of a bell, awoke me as we pulled into the station. Mrs. Watson, who had also fallen asleep, had set her hand just beside mine, almost touching, on the upholstered rest between our seats.

"Cambridge!" called the conductor from the narrow hallway.

On the short cab ride from the station to the university, Mrs. Watson asked me, "Since you say Professor Dirac's paper lays out his argument with clarity and precision, what, exactly, are we here to ask him?"

"We're not here to ask him anything," I answered.

She looked at me.

"We're here to warn him," I said.

❧

But we were too late.

A black wreath had been hung upon the locked door of Dirac's university rooms.

Mrs. Watson and I immediately made our way to the Department of Physics office, where the secretary, a young man with unruly hair and eyes of faintly different shades of green, recognized me.

"Professor von Schimmel," he said, standing up from behind his desk. "We didn't think we'd see you again. It's good to have you back. What a shame it's under these circumstances."

He assumed I'd returned to pay my respects.

"What happened to Dirac?" I asked, my German accent imperfect, betrayed by urgent concern.

"You don't know, Professor?"

I shook my head.

"Motoring accident," he said. "Poor man. So young. So brilliant."

I sat in a chair beside his desk. For the first time in my life I felt old. Not merely weary, nor saddened, nor alarmed, though I felt all those things as well. "Tell me more, please."

In brief, this is what he shared: Dirac had died in a single vehicle accident a few miles outside Cambridge two days before. There had been no other injuries and no witnesses. His automobile had struck an ancient oak. Dirac died from head trauma. Mrs. Watson put her hand on my arm, and I allowed her to keep it there. After a moment, I pressed the secretary for more, eventually regaining sufficient professional sangfroid to turn the conversation to the correspondence posted from this office and delivered just the day before to my Islington residence.

In this matter, the secretary's postal log proved helpful.

I learned that Professor Heinrich von Schimmel was not alone on Dirac's mailing list. The delivery to the Islington address was merely the most recent of three such postings that Dirac had instructed the department staff to complete. The other two dated from some weeks earlier, presumably upon Dirac's immediate completion of his paper.

The first carbon copy.

Sir Richard Gregory, editor of the distinguished scientific journal *Nature*. Placing a telephone call to the journal's editorial offices, I was not entirely surprised to learn that, like poor Dirac, Sir Richard had also died two days previous, he from a fall down a flight of stairs. Again, there had been no witnesses. Further, Dirac's final paper was no longer to be found in the journal's files, though there remained a carbon of an enthusiastic letter of acceptance written in Sir Richard's hand and dated two weeks previous. It is fortunate that Dirac's reputation was sufficient that his work had bypassed usual channels and gone straight to the top, thereby exposing no one else on the journal's editorial staff to danger. The same good fortune was true for the university staff, as Dirac had kept his research a closely guarded secret here. Two murders were quite enough.

The other carbon copy . . .

Surely, Dr. Watson would manage this revelation with more literary aplomb than I can muster.

I will simply state the fact.

The final copy went to His Majesty's government, in recognition of their financial support of Dirac's research at Cambridge; specifically, the mailing was posted to the government's most important senior operative: Mycroft Holmes, in care of the Diogenes Club, London.

Yes, my brother.

Unlike Dirac and Sir Richard, Mycroft was not dead. Rather, he was quite well. Nonetheless, I did not for a moment consider him uninvolved. Nor did I consider him to be in danger.

Most disconcerting.

In retrospect, I ought to have surmised it sooner.

❧

Big brother.

Naturally, Mycroft and I shared personal history as well as genes. But that is not the same as sharing constitution, ethos, or destiny, and, while some qualities of our minds and solitary habits aligned, we were always quite different from one another. Suffice to say that as boys our differences were best expressed by the old saw that familiarity breeds contempt. Meantime, the equally clichéd adage that absence makes the heart grow fonder has proven less accurate for us, judging from the long durations between our meetings over the years.

"What does your brother do?" Mrs. Watson asked.

By then, she and I were seated in the back of a hired car, motoring down the country road for London. Once back in the capital, we would relocate Conan Doyle from the Islington house, whose address, owing to the mailing list in the Cambridge department of physics, was likely known by now to the conspirators.

She continued: "I know from John's accounts that Mycroft works in the government. But doing what, these days?"

I glanced out my window. "At eighty, my brother maintains a uniquely powerful, if technically unspecified, position." The country-side looked less bucolic now than it had on the train ride up. I turned back to Mrs. Watson. "He 'fixes' problems for the Home Office, the Ministry of Defense, or any other governmental entity or interest deemed sufficiently important to occupy his valuable attentions."

"And what are the 'important interests' these days?" she asked.

I shook my head. "As I've been living a rather isolated, well-disguised life in academia these past few years, I've lost touch with the recent, secret workings of the government. Their concerns. I've lost touch with Mycroft, too. Our relations were never good."

"Why not?"

How to put this briefly . . . "He always thought I judged harshly the uses to which he put his intellect," I answered.

"Did you?"

"Yes."

"But he's worked for King and country."

"True. But who does King and country work for?"

She looked at me, waiting.

"The King's government . . ." I paused, turning the phrase over in my head. It was a misnomer, suggesting that the government belonged to the King rather than the other way around. I glanced into the front seat of our car. Was the driver listening to our conversation? His attention seemed focused on the road ahead. Perhaps too focused. No matter. Whether or not he was an agent, I'd speak my mind. "The King's government is little more than a well-greased financial concern, Mrs. Watson. The Empire is a multinational business. One might as well refer to the government, from the monarch down through the PM and Parliament, as the Bank of England. Or the England Company. It functions as little else."

She adjusted her skirts in her lap but did not seem put off by my less than patriotic assertion. Rather, she cut to the most immediate and personal consequence of what I'd just said—the danger. "I want you to know, Sherlock, that whatever happens, I'm glad to be along on this adventure. I mean, we're not working now to put an ordinary criminal behind bars or anything as mundane as that, true?"

"That's true."

She sat up straight and strong. "Well, I have no regrets, even if this is the last thing I do. *Particularly* if it's the last."

I didn't tell her how many times I had come to the same resolution at dangerous moments in previous cases. Nor did I tell her how often I'd felt vaguely disappointed when such endeavors turned in my favor and I was spared of the danger. Time and again, denied dying in an interesting manner. It was odd that now, being old, I held more tightly to my life. "We'll take no undue risks."

She smiled. "With you, I know that the word 'undue' is quite flexible. I've read John's accounts."

I began to defend myself, but she stopped me.

"Don't misunderstand, Sherlock. I wouldn't have it any other way."

"Good."

"I'm sorry about your friend, Dirac."

Was he my friend? Was I his friend? Dirac never knew my true identity. The Heinrich von Schimmel with whom he occasionally dined these past months was no less fictional than Oliver Twist. So, how could I consider myself to have been among Dirac's friends? Did he have other friends? I don't know. He was not gregarious. Indeed, he was socially inept. But he seemed to enjoy Von Schimmel's company. As I enjoyed his. I respected him. His untimely death represents a great loss to the world. Surely, I am sorry he is gone. Angry too. An empty space opened in my life where once there had been a man. Still, this didn't feel quite as it does when one loses a true friend. I'd experienced that once before in my life, and so I recognized well the difference.

CHAPTER TEN

That we should come now to two old men, brothers, sitting among the comfortable furnishings in the otherwise unoccupied visitors room of the Diogenes Club, the only room in the London gentlemen's club where speaking is allowed, may seem insufficient, both in setting and action, when compared to many of the dramatic climaxes that John chronicled in our cases. For example, the encounter with the great, red-eyed beast on the moors near Baskerville Hall, to say nothing of the bog itself, into which a man might, with one wrong step, sink to a slow, tortuous death; or, waiting in darkness and silence in the underground vault of the City and Suburban Bank for the dangerous John Clay to burst through the wall at the completion of his ingenious tunnel from the basement of an adjacent pawn shop; or the equally suspenseful anticipation, huddled in a young girl's deserted, candle-lit bedroom, of the appearance of a deadly snake, a speckled band, as it slithered down a rope pull to sink its fangs into the unsuspecting flesh that, absent our warning, would have lain abed. These are settings of inherent drama. Whereas the Diogenes Club is intended to provide quite the opposite of conflict or suspense. Founded by my brother, Mycroft, and a handful of other powerful men who cannot tolerate the relative sociability of other like clubs, the exclusive, comfortably appointed Diogenes Club provides its members with serenity that belies their professional lives, which, while appearing to be comprised of staid business or governmental administration, often consists instead of clandestine operations and manipulations in and of the greater world. Rumors hold that some members work for the King's intelligence services. I know this to be true, at least in the case of Mycroft. Of course, reference to any such endeavors is forbidden, along with spoken references to anything. No talking. Such brief and innocuous matters as when the footman is to bring a member another gin and tonic or single malt scotch are communicated with the merest gesture of the chin, absent even eye contact. The only sounds are the occasional tinkling of ice in tumblers or the crimpling of newspaper pages.

Before entering my brother's club, I stopped at a pub around the corner and slipped into the WC to change out of the disguise I had maintained in public since returning to London from Cambridge. Goodbye again to Professor von Schimmel. After my meeting with Mycroft there would be no further reasons to move about incognito, I suspected. Meanwhile, Mrs. Watson and Conan Doyle had taken refuge in my third and final safe house in London, a tiny flat near Madame Tussaud's, just around the corner from my old Baker Street residence. When I emerged from the WC in my own clothing and without the other accoutrements of disguise, I was recognized by a few of the pub patrons. Two or three asked to shake hands. I obliged, leaving a five pound note with the barkeep to cover a few rounds, and made it out the door before the back slapping or the "tell us how it really was" could begin. I crossed the busy street, attempting to comprehend the almost offensively counterintuitive proposition that in countless other simultaneous incarnations, lived, until now, exactly as I'd lived this life, I had just been run down by an almost infinite variety of carelessly driven motor cars, malfunctioning motor omnibuses, or ill-disciplined horse-drawn delivery wagons. It is enough to make one grateful for managing ever to cross a street alive, except that, statistically, there is a far greater number of cosmological instances in which one makes it across just fine. At least, such is my understanding of poor Dirac's theory.

"Understanding" is too definitive a word.

Doubtless, our brains are ill made for comprehending a continually branching and multiplying reality. This may be a result of natural selection, since grasping such a concept is of little practical use. One's life, after all, manifests as a singular line of narrative in what seems the only possible here and now, and that is all we can perceive, even if every possible outcome of every decision actually does occur *somewhere* in other versions of our own lives. To repurpose a term used in another context by the American philosopher William James, might we live in a *multiverse*? And, further complicating matters, mightn't there be an occasional crossing of the wires, a one-in-a-trillion random quantum fluctuation, wherein a ghostly image from an alternative universe actually makes a temporary appearance in ours, with or without the silly accoutrements of a séance? The crippled version of Stanley Baldwin, for example. For no reason at all. Indeed, this may happen more often than we know, as, absent context, we may not even recognize such temporary manifestations on the crowded streets for what they actually are, mistaking them for the ordinary.

Yes, I know this is claptrap. Of course I know.

But I know too that existence is claptrap.

So what do I know?

I tapped the knocker of the door to the unmarked Diogenes Club, located in the Pall Mall, announcing to the attendant that I was here to see Mycroft Holmes. The attendant nodded and showed me to the visitor's room, where I was alone only a moment before Mycroft entered.

"Well, Sherlock, I was wondering when you'd turn up here," he said.

Mycroft was still as rotund as I was lean.

I didn't stand to shake his hand as he closed the door behind him. Such formalities seem forced between brothers. At least, between us. Neither of us is inclined toward social niceties anyway. Nonetheless, Mycroft walked to my chair and, somewhat awkwardly, patted my shoulder. Then he crossed to the sofa across from the tea service and settled his large bulk into the cushions, arranging both the folds of the sofa and his own flesh until he was comfortable.

"Drink?" he asked.

"Scotch and soda," I said.

Mycroft reached to a side table and rang a bell.

Within seconds, a serving man entered.

"Two scotch and sodas," Mycroft instructed.

"Yes, sir." He closed the door softly after him.

"Is this your first visit to my club, Sherlock?"

"You know it's not, Mycroft."

"Yet still no application for membership? I'd be happy to sponsor you, little brother."

"I'm not the sociable type."

"Well, this is not a sociable club. You know that. It's nothing but silence in every other room."

"Rather like a mortuary," I commented.

He laughed, unpleasantly.

"Besides," I said, "I suspect that when it came time for a membership vote yours would be the only one I got."

"I wouldn't count on my vote either, Sherlock."

He looked healthy despite his excess weight. Perhaps living so completely in his mind allowed his body to balloon without deteriorating. Or, more likely, his wrinkles have simply been stretched to near invisibility. In either case, he looked little different than he'd looked twenty years before. Whereas I know my slender frame has not aged so invisibly. I no longer looked the younger brother.

"What kind of mischief have you gotten yourself into, Sherlock?" he asked, boring into me with his steel-grey, deep-set eyes. "Leading nocturnal escapades through the London sewers with that Conan Doyle chap? Just who did you think you were evading?"

"I can't say I know the names of the armed gentlemen who gave us chase. But I feel confident I know the name of the man they answer to, Mycroft."

"Did you come here to lodge a complaint?"

"Can't one simply call on his brother for the pleasure of keeping company?"

Mycroft smiled and then guffawed. "In theory, yes. In practice, for you and me, no. That is, unless things have changed between us. Recall, Sherlock, that you never even entered my bedroom when we were boys unless you had encountered some sort of enigma for which you required my assistance."

"That was because you set the terms of my ever entering your room. *Enigma required.*"

"And look where it's taken you, my dear little brother," he answered, without missing a beat.

"Yes, many unusual places."

"For example, here and now. Enigma still required," he said.

"I can supply that. But, of course, you already know."

He nodded. "How was it your late chronicler described me?"

"I don't precisely recall, Mycroft."

"I do."

"Well, you recall everything."

"Indeed." From memory, he quoted John's published description. "The conclusions of every government department are passed to Mycroft, and he is the central exchange, the clearinghouse, which makes out the balance. All other men are specialists, his specialism is omniscience . . . the government began by using him as a short-cut, a convenience; now he has made himself an essential. In that great brain of his everything is pigeon-holed and can be handed out in an instant."

"I'm glad John's writing is so memorable to you, Mycroft. He'd be gratified."

"Memorable to the whole dashed world," he murmured, stifling anger. "Do you realize what a nightmare such notoriety has made of my life? I can never enter a pub or restaurant without being grilled for all manner of information, from the next day's races at Ascot to the price of gold in Shanghai."

"But you never enter pubs or interact with strangers anyway," I said.

He considered. "I suppose you're right, Sherlock. As you so often are. But you didn't come here to discuss, let alone to apologize for, the particular brand of notoriety with which you have saddled me, have you?" He didn't wait for an answer. "Where *are* our whiskeys?" He glanced at the closed door as if he could conjure the footman at will.

And, indeed, the door opened just then.

The footman set the drinks before us.

"Thank you," Mycroft said, after which the footman turned and exited the room, closing the door behind him.

I picked up my drink and held it toward Mycroft, proposing a toast: "To enigmas." This was not the first time I'd toasted with a murderer. As previously noted, I am no unsullied hero in the manner of either the American Wild West or the romances of Sir Walter Scott. I am a professional. Expedience comes before all other concerns. Yes, lives had been taken. But it was my task to save the lives that remained threatened.

Mycroft raised his glass as well.

We were too distant to clink glasses, neither of us being willing to move for the other. But we both drank.

"Did you bring it, Sherlock?"

"It?" I inquired.

"A rather controversial academic paper recently posted from Cambridge University to the aforementioned, frightfully rundown Islington residence, which, according to my registry sources, is owned by . . . you."

I took a deep breath. "If you're referring to a fourteen-page typed document that may or may not be folded length-wise and carried now in the inside pocket of my coat, then, I suppose, the best answer I can offer is to cite recent experimental results from the vanguard of quantum mechanics that suggest not only the paradoxical conclusion that reality has no singular, independent existence but that what we perceive as real only comes into being when we observe it."

"The Copenhagen Interpretation," he murmured.

I nodded. "So, I suppose you could say that I both 'have' and 'don't have' the said document here in my pocket, dear brother."

"Conditions . . ." he grumbled. He spoke disdainfully now, as if to a common peddler. "You've come here to bargain, eh?"

"I refer to nothing so simple as bargaining."

"Everything is precisely that simple," he snapped. Then he gathered himself. "That is to say, everything is negotiable, dear brother."

"Negotiable until it's not," I answered. "Such as must have been the case with young Professor Dirac and Sir Richard Gregory, his editor. Those 'negotiations' came to abrupt conclusions indeed. If, that is, they ever even commenced."

Mycroft drank, savoring the liquor as it passed down his fleshy gullet. "How did Shakespeare put it?" He placed his drink on the end table and adjusted his posture, as if for a recitation. "Sometimes," he said, "conscience does *not* make cowards of us all, and thus the native hue of resolution is *not* sicklied o'er with the pale cast of thought, and enterprises of great pith and moment do *not* turn awry and do *not* lose the name of action."

"That's not how Shakespeare put it."

"Well, that's how I put it. And it's how the King's government puts it."

I said nothing.

He sighed and settled back into the cushions. "Oh, I will grant that it is sad indeed to lose two good Englishmen of science on the same day. Both so bright and enthusiastically forward looking."

I remained silent.

"But sometimes we men of action must *act*," Mycroft said.

As my brother's obesity makes his walking across a room something of a challenge, his claim to be a man of action might seem comically ironic. But it did not. There is nothing comical about Mycroft. Or his actions. So I changed the subject. "Frankly, I'm surprised you did not intercept this controversial document you speak of before it was delivered to my residence," I observed. "After all, you had access to the physics department mail log."

"Allow me to be honest with you, Sherlock, even if by doing so I may disillusion your impression of my omnipotence." He chuckled. "It's really frightfully simple. Our contact in Cambridge was sick in bed last week with a case of the grippe. As the physics department had mailed nothing of interest for quite some time, his absence didn't seem critical. So we missed that final mailing. Until yesterday. Yes, a mistake. Ah, for want of a nail and all that . . ."

"I've never believed you were omnipotent, dear brother."

He waved away the comment. "You're not here to talk about me,

Sherlock. You're too clever to waste my time or yours. No, you're here to talk about the future. True?" He didn't wait for an answer. "Unless there is some complication that I don't perceive."

"Complication?" I set my drink aside. "Well, the same experimental results that suggested the Copenhagen Interpretation to Bohr and Heisenberg recently suggested to the late Paul Dirac an alternative interpretation. Of course, you're already familiar with Dirac's postulate."

"Hmm ... My memory fails me. I'd like to hear you explain this alternative, Sherlock. Yes, this will be good. I want to hear you, a man of reason, speak ridiculous words."

"If *I* speak the words then they are not ridiculous."

He guffawed. "Your arrogance suggests you've confused your true self with that fictional abomination your old doctor friend created for the pulps."

"I've confused nothing."

"Fine, then tell me how the universe works, little brother."

"Simple. There may be more than one you, more than one me, more than one of everything." My words suggested more confidence in the theory than I truly possessed. But I'd learned long before that Mycroft tolerated no half measures. "Indeed, there may be countless iterations of all things, all existing simultaneously."

He chuckled. "You mean a world in which the greatest consulting detective is a German named Von Schimmel?"

I said nothing.

"Oh yes, our man in Cambridge returned from his illness yesterday," he continued. "Perhaps you remember him. Each eye a different shade of green. Unusual. Unfortunately, such physical distinctions limit an agent's prospects. In any case, who shows up in the physics department asking about the mail log? A Teutonic professor, accompanied by a woman we thereafter identified as a disguised Mrs. Watson, full of questions regarding the recent, tragic demise of poor Paul Dirac. This German is tall and lean, like you. It was not difficult to piece it all together, particularly as you'd been identified the night before upon your arrival in Bloomsbury." He made a tsk sound and shook his head before continuing. "In the interest of constructive criticism, I must add that your characterization of the German professor sounds quite over-wrought and far too reliant on cultural clichés. Sorry, dear boy."

Only Mycroft ever made me feel this way.

Not even Moriarty, who I'd killed for less.

I gathered myself, focusing on the matter at hand. With Mycroft it is important to strike back quickly and hard or not at all. "So, who's ridiculous now?"

"What do you mean?" he asked.

"It's you and your people who've given such credence to Dirac's outrageous theory of a multiplicity of universes that you killed him and his editor just to stop its dissemination." I allowed what I hoped would seem rational contempt to color my expression.

"His assertion cannot be disproved," he answered. "Perhaps that makes it something less than technically 'scientific.' But, at the same time, the assertion is enticing and seductive. So what's an active and responsible government to do?"

"The Copenhagen Interpretation."

"Yes, and that alone."

I took another drink.

He sighed and somehow managed to sink even deeper into the sofa. "Dear Sherlock, this whole quantum mechanics business is without practical application for 99.999 percent of our citizens. However, the philosophical implications may not prove so rarified. Nor the moral ones. And it's this government's job to maintain order. Consider the implications of this question: can it be that even *I* am a criminal in some other universe? If such a thing were so, then why oughtn't I to place my own well-being ahead of law, decency, and the public good in this universe as well? Do you not see the danger of such thinking among the criminally inclined?"

"You've already been a criminal in this world, Mycroft. For years."

"Or," he continued, ignoring my observation, "reversing the equa-tion, if I am a law-abiding citizen in another universe, then what responsibility to the law do I have here? It doesn't matter if this quantum branching of universes is or is not an accurate description of reality. What matters is that it may be interpreted by those inclined but not yet committed to lawlessness as license to commit crime, perversion, or even atrocities. And, worse yet, imagine what would happen to Imperial power in the colonies if the masses ever came to believe that in one universe or another they will inevitably do every possible thing under every possible circumstance, including overthrowing their British superiors? Why then would they be inclined to follow our rules here and now?"

"The Empire thing," I murmured. "The doomed obsession of you and yours."

"The Empire is not doomed, merely threatened," he snapped. "That is why it must be deliberately handled."

"And this many-worlds theory . . ." I started.

He interrupted: "Potentially catastrophic."

"There are Buddhists living under our rule in Burma today who have embraced just such notions for thousands of years, absent the scientific rationale," I indicated. "And Hindus in India."

"Yes, and they often present authorities with grave disrespect."

"No doubt warranted," I said.

He shifted his weight among the cushions. "You have a right to your political views, Sherlock. But that's only because the government allows it." He stopped. "Well, we generally allow it. I suppose you wouldn't be here now if there were no limits to what one may think or say or write. Nonetheless, you are free to criticize Imperial power because to do so has no direct cost to you. Why? Because *you* do not shoulder the responsibility for an empire weakened by the events of the past few decades. Believe me, it is no soiree. For this reason, I have always envied you, little brother. Serving only your own intellectual fascinations even as you cultivate your self-aggrandizement."

"You underestimate the value of my life's work, brother," I said.

"As you underestimate the value of mine."

For a moment, we were silent.

Then Mycroft sighed, as weary of the old resentments as I. "It is simple," he said, returning to our current conflict. "The King's government, in addition to other clear-thinking European governments who are also involved in international trade and statecraft, foresee negative consequences if seemingly 'irrational' thinking is ever confused with 'modern science.'"

I looked at him. "It's not the 'science' that frightens you and others of your ilk," I observed. "Nor criminality, nor even politically inspired upheaval."

Once again, his ugly chuckle. "Nothing frightens me, Sherlock. This is because our Empire, which you demean so lightheartedly, can deal with all things."

I shook my head. "You can't deal with God."

"What?" He broke into laughter. "God? And this coming from you, Sherlock? That's rich!"

"Your millions of subjugated Hindus would explain it like this." I quoted from memory the *Bhagavata Purana*. "Even though over a period of time I might count all the atoms of the universe, I could not count all my opulence, which I manifest within *innumerable universes*."

He leaned back in the cushions. "Ah, the fruit of your 'missing years' spent east of Suez. Your cross-legged meditating in monasteries. And now you consider yourself expert in all things Eastern. Hah!"

I ignored his deprecation. "And in the *Apannaka Jataka*, the Buddha refers to the 'lowest of hells below and the highest heaven above and all the *infinite worlds* that stretch right and left.'"

He picked up his drink and finished it. Then he returned the glass to the end table. "Well, there's a passing grade for the second form student of theology."

"Not much has changed since the first incarnation of the Eureka Society," I observed. "That covert corps of fanatics Rome organized to assassinate Poe, a mere literary unfortunate."

"What, that shadowy papal conspiracy from the last century?" he objected. "Rome was frightened by mere philosophizing. They were disorganized and emotional. Not British at all."

"It is not merely the name that you've adopted," I said.

"No, what else have we taken from the papists?"

"It is still about God."

"That's absurd, Sherlock. The King's government is not a tool of the Church."

"No, the Church is a tool of yours," I replied. "A tool that has proven useful to all the Western Powers. But what would happen if millions of brown-skinned people were to learn that *their* religions more neatly align than do ours with the boldest and most current incarnation of the very cudgel we now wield against them, science? What if *we* are the primitives?"

"What would happen?" Mycroft snapped. "Probably nothing."

"*Probably* nothing," I answered. "We both know that 'probably' is not a word that you and yours have ever been willing to tempt."

His manner softened and he leaned back. "I suppose I could argue with your assertions, little brother. But why should I bother, as you so neatly, if inadvertently, have just made the case for my government's unrestrained involvement in this matter. If I stipulate that what you say is true, what need I further do?"

I hadn't an answer for him.

"So what does that leave?" he pressed.

"Your modern incarnation of the Eureka Society," I said.

He stared at me long enough to communicate an affirmative answer. Then he said without conviction, "I've never heard of such an organization."

"Just as you never heard of a blond assassin recently shot through the right lung outside the offices of the Society for Psychic Research?"

Now, he could not hide his surprise. After a moment, comprehension spread across his wide face. "Ah, *you* were the East Indian psychic and the tippler with the gun!" He shook his head in seeming delight. "I should have guessed it."

I did not answer but allowed my silence to affirm his statement.

"You've been quite busy, Sherlock," he observed.

"As have you, Mycroft."

"Oh, I don't condone killing," he said, shifting as if suddenly uncomfortable in the sofa cushions in which he now half reclined. I wondered if he'd be able to stand up out of the soft fabric divot without help. "But then, dear Sherlock, it's not my place to condone *or* condemn. I am a mere servant of the Crown."

"And what of Conan Doyle, a good man and also a loyal servant of the Crown?"

"He is a frightfully loose cannon who is also a professional writer. A dangerous combination."

"A writer of mere historical romances and dinosaur fantasies," I objected.

Mycroft pursed his heavy lips. "I agree that his oeuvre *should* disqualify him from serious cultural consideration or influence. To say nothing of some of his previous civic causes, each more embarrassing to him than the last. However, the public does not necessarily concur with our assessment, dear brother." He grew more animated. "Unfortunately, Conan Doyle was knighted for his history of the Boer War. This is not insignificant. It lends him weight with the public. Yet it does nothing, in our view, to make him more trustworthy. Do you understand our dilemma?" He didn't wait for an answer. "Conan Doyle is evangelical in his beliefs and will continue to publicly assert his fleeting encounter with an 'alternate' Stanley Baldwin. He may not tie the appearance to any quantum theory, being unaware of the new science. But if others put things together?"

"The bullet lodged near his spine put a caution in him."

"Did it? Just a few days ago he attempted to post an essay regarding the subject."

"He did not associate the two events, having missed the 'message' implied by his shooting."

Mycroft shook his head. "Oh, we could clarify our demands. This would frighten him temporarily. But we know his type. His pride will not allow him ever to stand down. He may *seem* to concede. For years even. Yet he also may make a secret provision in his will for an exposé to run in newspapers at the time of his death. That sort of nonsense. So, for that reason, threatening him is a poor strategy, which I say as something of a compliment to him, whatever his fate."

In that moment, I thought it would have been better to have thrown my own brother rather than Moriarty over the Reichenbach Falls. "I shall not tell you where to find Conan Doyle," I said.

"You'd be withholding evidence from the Crown."

"He hired me to save his life . . . from you."

"Not I, Sherlock. The government."

"But you are the government."

He chuckled. "You overestimate me. Those days have passed. I'm now only the third or fourth most powerful man in England."

I finished my scotch and soda.

"We've located your latest safe house," Mycroft announced. "The one near your old Baker Street rooms."

Suddenly, I could have used a second drink. "What, how?"

"Mrs. Watson was spotted by one of our agents as she was buying eggs at a grocery this morning. Good fortune for us. Our man followed her back to the residence. Now, it's time for the grown-ups of this world, however many *other* worlds there may or may not be, to put an end to the problem."

"The two are still safe?"

He nodded. "As I suspected you'd seek me out, I waited to talk with you before ordering any action."

"Why?"

"Isn't it answer enough that you're my brother?"

"No."

He leaned forward on the sofa until he managed to pull himself half out of the valley of fabric. "I wanted to consult with you because Conan Doyle is no longer the only influential person in possession of this radical and politically, culturally, and spiritually threatening theory."

I pretended slow-wittedness. "You're talking about Madam Du Lac?"

He brushed the suggestion away with his hand. "She's a psychic medium, for God's sake. She can say whatever she wants. Her word carries no weight."

"But Conan Doyle is a proponent of Spiritualism. Why not allow him the same charitable insignificance?"

"Because being a proponent and being a medium are two different things," he answered. "There are many influential personages who take an interest in the ridiculous confidence games played out in séance rooms. Even some in the royal family, I'm sorry to say. So, you see, *Sir* Arthur Conan Doyle is not dismissed so easily."

I said nothing, waiting.

"And your Mrs. Watson could pose something of a threat should she begin talking," he continued.

I shook my head dismissively. "She was a mere landlady until she married Watson." I hoped to defend her by defaming the genuinely formidable woman I'd come to know. "I don't see the slightest distinction in anything she's ever done. Nor would the general public. She's no threat to you."

"But she *is* a respectable woman," Mycroft countered. "And, as you say, she was married to a literary man."

"She has no intention of taking any of this information to the public."

He shrugged. "Of course, there's a chance that what you say is true. Indeed, a likelihood. But with the stakes so high . . ."

"You'll not harm her," I said, firmly.

He laughed. "Oh, *I'll* harm no one, Sherlock. Just look at me. I am not a model of modern British physical fitness."

"If harm comes to her I'll kill you myself, Mycroft."

"Ah yes, that brings us to you, doesn't it." Despite the syntax, his words did not constitute a question.

I extended my arms and held my fists out toward him, as if for handcuffs. "Call your men and take me right away to Reading Gaol, or wherever it is you put men of public acclaim these days. Or call your retired military specialists to take me to a private place in the woods and do their worst."

He indicated with a motion of his hands for me to put my arms down. "I'm your *brother*, Sherlock," he said, as if offended by my callous suggestions. "I would never sign off on your arrest or assassination. Unless, that is . . ." He stopped, saving the breath it would have taken him to complete the sentence, leaving it to me.

"Unless I give you no choice," I said.

"Exactly. However, before we go any further, I want to make something perfectly clear. I didn't know you were the East Indian mystic in Kensington, so I hope you don't hold that one against me. I'm truly glad you got the best of our man."

I shrugged. "A mere bygone."

"I'm going to offer you a deal, Sherlock. It's . . ."

"I've come with a proposal of my own," I interrupted. I'd learned as a boy never to let Mycroft set the initial parameters of a negotiation. Nothing in all the years since had dissuaded me from the discipline.

"All right, Sherlock. What do you want?"

"I need access to the finest photography lab in the country, tonight. With a technician whose discretion is beyond reproach. Additionally, I'll need materials that are currently housed at the British Museum delivered to the lab by an equally trustworthy courier. Finally, I'll need government stationery, a typewriter, and seals that would pass inspection. And then a week to put my plan into full effect. You can continue to surveil us, so there'll be no mischief. If, after that date, you are dissatisfied, then you can take whatever actions you deem to be in the government's interest. Sans guilt."

"And this will discharge my problem?"

"Yes, Mycroft."

"And you'll hand over your copy of Dirac's paper, there in your pocket?"

I nodded.

"Photography lab," he mused. "Seven days. That doesn't seem to be asking so much. Not for my only brother. But let's make it six days. Considering the Lord created the universe, or perhaps a multitude of them, in such time, it ought to be enough time for you, dear Sherlock. For whatever you have in mind."

"Fine."

"Of course, I have a few minor stipulations of my own."

CHAPTER ELEVEN

Perhaps in some *univers parallèles* Mrs. Watson, Conan Doyle, and I made a furtive escape that night, shortly after my return from the Diogenes Club. This escape may have been preceded by our calmly toasting the bold endeavor with bubbling flutes of *Dom Pérignon*, 1921, and my announcement, with more than a little of Douglas Fairbanks's aplomb, to my two fugitive companions: "Of course we have a way out of our predicament!" Whereupon, climbing once more down into the labyrinthine sewers of London, an exciting chase would ensue, with agents of the Crown hot on our trail, firing their weapons, bullets coming near enough to rain shattered pieces of wood and concrete from the sewer construction near to our shadowed, fleeing figures. As Victor Hugo put it when he sent his characters into the Paris sewers for their miraculous escape, "Adorable ambuscades of providence!" Ultimately, we rise and emerge from the sewer *within* the walls of Buckingham Palace, my mental map of the underground web of passageways being perfect, and we make our way, stealthily, past the King's Guard to the private chambers of the royal family, where, slipping into the very bedroom of our monarch, we wake him and explain the situation, of which he knows nothing. Outraged, he calls for an immediate, midnight gathering of his counsel and, the next morning, announces that some of those whose charge is to work on His Royal behalf, including Mycroft, have failed to do the King's true bidding, as the monarch is a proponent of truth in whatever form it takes, disavowing the antiscientific, socially manipulative intelligence forces who've pursued us. The rest, then, would become global history, as, freed from political pressures, Dirac's surviving colleagues would publicly assert alternative theories to the Copenhagen Interpretation, eventually finding scientific proof of the startling reality of multiple worlds, revolutionizing human thought. Allow me to add an exclamation point to that last phrase: revolutionizing human thought!

Of course, this is not what happened.

At least not in this universe. Nor, according to the theory, in all but an almost infinitesimally small minority of universes.

In the only world I know, it happened like this:

The morning after my negotiation with Mycroft, I arrived back at my final safe house. I carried a new leather valise under my arm. Mrs. Watson and Conan Doyle sat at table for breakfast. Eggs. I didn't tell Mrs. Watson how costly her going to the market to buy those eggs had proven. But perhaps having undercover government men stationed outside the residence made no difference anymore. We hadn't planned to conceal ourselves forever. Some resolution was always required. Of course, I could explain none of the details to my companions, particularly to the ever-enthusiastic raconteur Conan Doyle, whose soon-to-be ruined reputation was key to saving his life.

"Good morning, Sherlock," Mrs. Watson said as I entered, as if I were her night-watchman husband returning home from an ordinary shift.

Conan Doyle sat at the table, sipping tea. He looked up at me with wide eyes. "What news, my good man?"

I set the leather valise on the table.

"You've been out all night," Mrs. Watson observed.

"Yes."

"Good Heavens," she said. "Sit down and let me get you a cup of tea."

I sat down. And I'd take the tea.

"Eggs?" she asked.

I shook my head.

Though I'd developed affection for both of my companions, Conan Doyle for his brave heart and Mrs. Watson for her devotion and outstanding mind, the domesticity of the scene nonetheless went against my nature, practically making my skin crawl; I'm not proud of this reaction, but I cannot recall a time, even in childhood, when family-like matters inspired in me any other response. Perhaps having introduced you, dear reader, to my brother, Mycroft, goes some way toward an explanation. And there was more. Consider yourself fortunate to be spared description of my father's violently demanding conduct in the family house. Suffice to say that at age seven I was greatly relieved to be sent away to boarding school. And the past was not the only source of my discomfort that morning among my covert flatmates. I also found the casual trappings of the overly familiar kitchen scene to be in ill-keeping with the actual seriousness of the situation. But I could display none of my discomfort, as this was to be a scene in a drama, which, if produced properly, would result in the survival of its unknowing *dramatis personae*.

"Well, man, what have you learned?" Conan Doyle asked, leaning across the wooden table toward me.

"The government is involved," I answered.

He nodded. "As we suspected."

Mrs. Watson turned away from the stove, setting a steaming cup of tea before me and pulling a chair to join us at the table.

"So the manifestation was real?" Conan Doyle pressed.

I shook my head. "It was a trick," I said. "The *actual* prime minister took part. An experiment. The three-dimensional, semi-transparent effect was achieved with a new technology consisting of film projectors and carefully placed mirrors. That our PM *appeared* to be crippled was the work of make-up and special effects experts, including the American film star Lon Chaney."

Conan Doyle's face dropped. "Your brother in the government told you this?"

"Indeed," I said, though of course he'd said no such thing.

Mrs. Watson looked unconvinced.

"But the manifestation spoke to me!" Conan Doyle insisted. "Not only that, but he knew where to find you. How?" His tone of voice changed.

"The government has ways of keeping track of a man, even when he's well enough disguised that all others lose his trail."

Conan Doyle considered. "So . . . why would this illusory manifestation direct me to call on you?"

"For the experiment," I said, realizing only as I spoke how thin my story was becoming. John would have created a more convincing narrative, even from whole cloth. Of course, he'd never written fiction, claiming that he'd had no need thanks to our professional engagements.

"But I was shot!" Conan Doyle said, standing from the table.

Mrs. Watson also stood and put her hand comfortingly on his shoulder.

I shrugged. "The government had nothing to do with your shooting," I said. "It must have been an ordinary criminal. Who knows?"

"You expect me to believe that?" he demanded.

"And the attack on you in the garden of the Society for Psychic Research?" Mrs. Watson objected, quite reasonably.

"London is a dangerous city," I offered. "Open spaces after dark . . ."

"And the men lingering outside the Bloomsbury house?" Mrs. Watson continued.

"Perhaps mere vagrants."

"And the deaths of Dirac and his editor?" Conan Doyle inquired.

"Accidents, both."

"You expect us to believe coincidences like that?" Conan Doyle demanded, nervously tightening and loosening his fists.

"You think the odds longer for accidents or street crime than for that of a spectral appearance from a parallel universe?" I responded, dismissively.

Both appeared full of doubt. I didn't blame them.

I do not make a habit of lying. Disguise, artifice, misdirection, contrivance, yes. These are tools with which I am not merely familiar, but expert. However, lying like this to my own client, Conan Doyle, and to Ms. Watson, effectively my partner on this case, was different. I didn't like it. But what choice did I have? I needed to gauge Conan Doyle's reaction. His potential willingness to let go of the wonder he had expe-rienced. In that regard, I suppose, the lies proved effective.

"No!" Conan Doyle insisted. "I will not believe you, Holmes. I saw what I saw. And I heard the voice and felt the warm breath of the crip-pled Baldwin's spirit in my ear. It was no trick of film projection and mirrors. I know how that fraudulent business is done. Do you think me a fool?"

I shook my head but managed no words before he continued, growing further enraged.

"Your brother in government bought you off, Holmes," he insisted. "I see that now. I don't know what he gave you, but he's turned you. Goddamn you, Holmes. Don't think my account to the newspapers won't expose this. All of it."

Any such account to the newspaper would not only fail ever to be published but would also serve as his death warrant.

He started from the room.

My course of action had been determined. "Wait!" I called.

Conan Doyle had made his determination clear. Also clear was that his life was more important than his reputation. I knew he'd likely disagree, being a man of honor, but I suspected his family would align on my side, though they would never know it had come down to one or the other. "You haven't asked what I have in the satchel, Conan Doyle," I offered, picking it up from the table.

"What is it?" he ventured.

"What may have seemed wondrous to us before, whether false or true, was mere prologue," I said. "What I do or do not believe about the manifestation of the alternate Stanley Baldwin is irrelevant now. What I have here changes everything."

He took a step toward the table.

"Sit down, Conan Doyle. Mrs. Watson." As they once again took chairs, I opened the satchel.

This is not about winged fairies.

Nonetheless, I beg your patience. I know that this narrative already strains credulity in the manner with which it treats the unprovable assertion that there may be more than one me, more than one you, more than one world, indeed, that there may be literally countless versions of everything in existence. I don't know what I'd make of reading such jabberwocky myself. Or perhaps I do know what I'd make of it.

So, I do not bring up fairies lightly, as my reliability as narrator may already be suspect.

Fairies are, indeed, the last thing I can imagine offering to win your trust.

Nonetheless, it is fairies that lead us to our conclusion.

Some years ago, Conan Doyle became involved professionally in the case of a pair of sisters, mere girls from a Yorkshire village, who claimed to have photographed fairies in the woods behind their home. Tiny, humanoid creatures with wings. I knew of Conan Doyle's association with the ludicrous story only because Dr. Watson happened upon it one morning in the back pages of the newspaper as we took tea in our rooms at Baker Street. He recognized Conan Doyle's name from the minor legal entanglement the two had endured long before over the issue of plagiarism in Conan Doyle's short story "B.24." John and I indulged in some uncharitable chuckling over Conan Doyle's spirited defense of the fairy photographs.

Don't get me wrong. I do not believe in fairies and neither should you.

When the young girls' photographs were adjudged by the public to be frauds, the story subsided, and Conan Doyle turned his attention elsewhere. His reputation was not much besmirched, primarily because his argument for the girls and their encounter with fairies had gained so little attention. After all, his name was then still somewhat obscure, having not yet achieved the renown that came with the publication of his most recent novel, *The Lost World*, and the attendant exposure created by its successful cinema adaptation. See real dinosaurs! Since the success, he'd devoted his journalistic and public speaking efforts to the support of Spiritualism, which enjoys a more popular and, if I may be allowed to use the word loosely, respectable status among the public than ever have winged fairies. This is why his journalistic reputation, at the time of these events, was largely rehabilitated. This, of course, also accounted for the particular attention he'd garnered from my brother and his ilk. Hence the bullet near his spine, which had been intended to kill.

My suspicion about the assassination attempt on my unknown East Indian mystic, Siddhartha Singh, who carried no such cultural weight as Conan Doyle, was that the current incarnation of the Eureka Society may have suspected the two were working together and had concluded that there was no sense taking any chances, there being no downside to the murder of an immigrant anyway.

In any case, I knew now that I could never dissuade Sir Arthur from attempting to publish his account of the manifestation of an alternative, crippled version of our still-living PM. He was nothing if not brave.

So I'd chosen this other tack.

"What's in the satchel?" Conan Doyle asked, settled once more at the kitchen table. His tone remained disgruntled with my apparent betrayal, but his curiosity would not allow him to ignore possibilities.

Mrs. Watson watched silently. I did not look at her, but I felt her eyes on me.

I knew she was confused, but I also knew she still trusted me.

I removed from the satchel a pile of papers; some were typed and stamped with official government seals, while others were merely handwritten notes. Additionally, I removed a half dozen photographs. I placed it all facedown on the table. "While in Mycroft's private office, he left me alone for a short time, during which I took the opportunity to peruse his desk and files." Mycroft had no private office, besides the Diogenes Club, but neither Conan Doyle nor Mrs. Watson could know that for sure. My entire technique was narrowing now to dissimulation. I thought of Hemingway's assertion in Paris that the nearest thing to being a writer was being a detective and vice versa. He'd meant it in a different sense. But I'd been creating a fiction all morning. Surely,

John would have recommended I document here some more heroic way to save my companions than simply falsifying photographs, but, as I have said frequently on these pages, *I am not John*. He is irreplaceable to me. Besides, this is how it happened.

"Did you find something in your brother's office?" Mrs. Watson asked.

"I found nothing relating to the case at hand. That's why I had nothing to report, except the litany of denial and rationalization as it was given to me by Mycroft. You may blame me, Sir Arthur, but I only passed on to you what I was told, plausible or not. Believe what you will. I too have doubts about my brother's testimony. However, in his brief absence from his office, I found something even more intriguing than any unconventional spirit manifestation." I indicated the documents and the facedown photographs. "I slipped these out of his office, unbeknownst to him."

Both Conan Doyle and Mrs. Watson leaned over the table, nearer the documents.

I flipped the pictures over.

"Ah," Conan Doyle said, immediately recognizing the photograph atop the pile.

It was of a young girl in a woodland keeping company with winged fairies the size of a man's hand.

"Mycroft had this?" Conan Doyle asked.

"Yes," I lied. "In a file marked Top Secret."

Mycroft would never be so careless. But Conan Doyle's rich and ever optimistic imagination made him among the most gullible men I'd ever met, and Mrs. Watson was following my lead, without need for explanation, out of an unspoken trust that I found both reassuring and reminiscent of her late husband.

"Amazing!" Conan Doyle exclaimed, turning over the next photograph.

It ought to have struck him as such, seeing as I'd spent all night in the finest lab in the realm, working with the King's own photographer, to produce the trick images based on the original, primitive attempt at special-effects photography undertaken by the young girls themselves back in '17. Indeed, we'd produced photographs impossible to imagine coming from mere village children more than a decade before, unless, of course, the photographs were authentic. What had appeared in the girls' original photographs, to all but the most credulous eye, as mere, two dimensional cut-outs of magazine images of fairies flitting about, now appeared as fully three dimensional; the tiny creatures' wings were even slightly blurred by manipulation of the photographic plates. It was a masterful counterfeit of reality.

Too bad they would never see the light of day, their sole display being limited to this room.

"But these photos . . ." Conan Doyle muttered.

"They're crystal clear," Mrs. Watson observed. "The fairies are three dimensional."

"Not like before," Conan Doyle continued, flipping to the next photograph, which was also of the girl and the fairies.

The pictures would likely have fooled Cecil Beaton.

"I know it's been some years now since your support for the girls in Cottingley and their photographs, but perhaps it's not too late to redeem what must seem something of an indignity in your otherwise distinguished journalistic record," I suggested to Conan Doyle, who perused the last of the photographs in wonder.

"But these are not the photos!" he exclaimed. "I mean, in the years since I championed the girls' pictures it became obvious, even to me, that I'd been taken in by fakes. I never thought I'd want to revisit the incident. But these pictures . . . What goes on here?"

"These *are* the girls' actual photos from 1917," I lied. "They were confiscated, reworked, and replaced with the images presented to you and others. At the time, of course, even the diminished images were deemed sufficiently evidentiary. At least, by some."

Conan Doyle shrugged. "By me, for example."

"And by the girls themselves, who were too young to realize that their actual photographs had been replaced and that they were being played as frauds."

"But what objection could the powers that be have to fairies?" he asked.

This question crossed too far into the absurd. "I have no answer for that, Sir Arthur."

"But these photographs constitute proof that will stand up to scrutiny!" he said.

"Yes, proof, which, allow me to remind you, does *not* exist for your mere testimonial regarding the manifestation of an 'alternate' Stanley Baldwin," I added.

He shuffled through the authentic-looking documentation, his heavily lined face alight. "After the publication of these photographs, along with my account of the conspiracy and my renewed argument for the existence of other-dimensional entities sharing our Earth, namely what we refer to as 'fairies,' the public will be more trusting of what I must admit is, indeed, a mere testimonial about the Stanley Baldwin affair. In short, they'll be more trusting of me."

Of course, the effect would be just the opposite.

"How quickly can you complete your article to accompany these photographs?" I inquired. "I worry that Mycroft may discover the file missing and confiscate everything before you can submit the package to the newspapers."

"I'm a very fast writer when I need to be."

"In this instance, you need to be," I said.

Mrs. Watson watched the exchange wordlessly.

That afternoon, we each left the safe house for the comforts of our own residences. I knew we were still under surveillance, but such knowledge was not necessary for my former companions. They were free to go about their business. Such was the bargain, at least for the next six days. When I reached my own London rooms I fell into a deep sleep, not awakening until the next evening. Apparently, Conan Doyle needed no such rest but had gotten straight to work.

I am not altogether proud of what followed.

But my charge was to save the man's life, not his public reputation.

Within forty-eight hours of our leaving the last safe house, Conan

Doyle had completed his article asserting that fairies were real, whatever doubts the public expressed when he'd first made such an assertion years before, and he submitted the writing to the *Times* of London along with the corroborating photographs. The next day, an article ran under the headline "Well Known Author Losing His Mind?" Conan Doyle's arguments had been excerpted within the larger article, which publicly challenged Sir Arthur's sanity. Such a charge seemed justified, as the photographs published alongside the damning article were not the meticulous works of prestidigitation that the King's photographer and I had created a few nights before but the original 1917 photos, which were even more obviously fakes now than they'd been the first time Conan Doyle publicly supported them. Naturally, Mycroft had important connections at the *Times*. The switch doubtless had been easily achieved. Enraged, Conan Doyle responded with a letter to the editor stating that these were *not* the photographs he had submitted with his article. The letter made him seem only more unstable. Now, he could shout from the pulpit of St. Paul's that a manifestation of an alternate Stanley Baldwin had appeared to him during a séance, and he would draw no more than a bemused or perhaps piteous response from the public.

I ruined him.

I saved him.

His wife returned from the Continent; his children visited, bringing to him his grandchildren in hopes of restoring him to sanity.

From all family accounts, it worked.

But his public life was over.

Mycroft was satisfied, except, of course, as regarded what was to become of me.

✑

No arrests ever were made. I achieved justice for neither the shooting of Conan Doyle nor for the murders of Paul Dirac and Sir Richard Gregory. Nor did I either overturn the British government or enlighten the world with a new quantum possibility. Perhaps you are disappointed in the indefatigable Sherlock Holmes; after all, until now you have only known of me through John's accounts, which were restricted to those cases that offered exactly the satisfactions of villains punished and truth restored.

Once more I remind you that this is real.

Choices had to be made.

Sorry.

❧

The day of the *Times* article, I called on Mrs. Watson at her Belgravia address. The house where John had lived his final days. The house in which he'd died. She welcomed me as if it were my house now, too.

But it was not.

The weather was lovely, so we passed through the residence to the small back garden, settling beside one another on a comfortable bench overhung by a hawthorn tree. Her housemaid brought the sterling silver tea set, which she set on a fashionably weathered wooden table before us. Then the girl left.

"Shall I pour, Sherlock?" Mrs. Watson asked.

"Yes, please."

I didn't know how much explanation Mrs. Watson would require, nor if she would approve of my manipulations. "It's a hard day for Sir Arthur," I observed, taking from her the proffered cup and saucer.

"Yes, but he's safe now."

She seemed to require little or no explanation.

"Still, I found it difficult to stomach the newspaper this morning," I said.

She nodded and then sipped her tea. "A quite comprehensive condemnation."

"He's a proud man, despite his history of credulous analysis when it comes to various esoterica," I continued.

"True, but he's safe now," she repeated.

"For whatever that's worth."

She looked at me, confused. "In the case of Sir Arthur, that's worth quite a lot."

"Oh, of course," I answered. "He's a fine man."

She leaned toward me, as if what she were about to say was private. "I believe I understand the quite clever part you've played in this fairy business, Sherlock. And I want you to know that I heartily approve."

"Good," I said. "But I'm not sure that I approve of it."

"What?"

"Upon reflection, I'm not sure it mightn't have been kinder to let the government assassins take him."

"You can't mean that."

"Mightn't his good name be more important to him than his life?"

She set her tea down on the wooden table. When she spoke, it was with friendly certitude. "I think you're mistaking your own values for his, Sherlock. It's *you* who would rather die than be proven incompetent. Or even wrong. I imagine that's why John only ever wrote about the cases you solved."

"Well, we did solve most of them."

She smiled. "Look, Conan Doyle asked you to save his life. And you did."

His was not the only life I had saved by my irksome dealings with Mycroft. But I said nothing more about that.

"And you identified the guilty party, even if the government and its agents remain beyond punishment," she continued.

"Yes, but I didn't 'get to the bottom of it,' as I assured Conan Doyle I'd do."

She edged forward on her seat. "I'm not sure there *is* a bottom to it," she said.

"Mrs. Watson, I have not made my name by accepting such premises."

She sighed. "You're asking yourself how Conan Doyle found you in Cambridge." She exhibited an impressive native capacity for what Dupin called *ratiocination*. "That whole alternate PM business?"

I nodded. "The finest minds in the realm were taken in by my various disguises. So how did Conan Doyle, innocent that he is, turn up in the rooms of Professor von Schimmel? Unless, of course..." I stopped, wearied of voicing speculation that sounded like H. G. Wells after a night of drinking.

But Mrs. Watson picked up my aborted sentence without losing a beat. "Unless an 'alternate' Stanley Baldwin actually contacted Conan Doyle in the séance room," she proposed. "A Stanley Baldwin who somehow knew of your disguise and where you were to be found."

I shrugged in acknowledgement.

"But how would any such person have known?" she asked. "Particularly if he existed in . . . well, in another world."

I'd asked myself the same question. "Among a countless number of worlds, there would be some in which the secret identity of another Sherlock Holmes, also disguised as a Cambridge visiting lecturer named Von Schimmel, would be known, perhaps through routine means, to a crippled, never elected prime minister version of Stanley Baldwin. Of course, such scenarios are highly unlikely. However, they also would be virtually inevitable if the number of universes were large enough."

"And Dirac's theory proposes the number may be that great?"

"Yes."

"But why would *that* Stanley Baldwin share information about your whereabouts with *our* Conan Doyle?" she asked.

"Mistaken identity, perhaps," I answered. "In various alternate scenarios, Conan Doyle and I might have a multitude of relationships, many different from the one we have here. Friends, enemies, who can imagine all the possibilities? And in such circumstances they'd all be not only possible but inevitable."

She narrowed her eyes. "I *think* I follow your reasoning."

"It's not my reasoning, but inferences from Dirac's proposal."

"But... even if all this is so, how could there be contact between such universes?"

From my reading on quantum mechanics, I had picked up a few phrases. *Random quantum fluctuation*, for one. The predictable, inevitable occurrence of the altogether unpredictable. In other words, unreasonable, illogical, seemingly impossible accidents. But where and when such accidents might occur is impossible to predict, as quantum mechanics plays havoc with determinism. Would that do as an answer for Mrs. Watson? Likely not, as it raises a question that offended even as adventurous an intellect as Einstein's: does Nature play dice? And does it play with dice that are not merely six-sided but of a countless number of sides, rolling countless games and thereby every possible combination? No, Mrs. Watson was a reasonable woman. And this was not, in any ordinary sense, a "reasonable" answer, even if it could be true.

"How?" she repeated, emphatic.

"Ay, there's the rub," I said, having long ago discerned that quoting Shakespeare, even meaninglessly, proves a safe bet when you've no adequate response to a good question.

She didn't lower her eyes from mine. "So, do you believe Dirac's theory is true?"

"*Univers parallèles*?" The phrase seemed less offensive to common sense when spoken in French.

"Yes, do you believe it?"

"Believe, hmmm . . ." I no longer felt compelled to lecture Mrs. Watson on the irrelevancy of what I did or did not believe. Particularly as the question no longer felt irrelevant. So, I answered her. "Dirac's speculation is well-argued and is consistent with scientific observation. It's as 'reasonable' as the Copenhagen Interpretation. But, for all that, it is speculation. So, it cannot be taken as a fact. Even if . . ." I stopped.

"If what?"

"Even if I wish it could."

She sat back. "*Wish*," she mused. "That's an odd word coming from you."

Indeed, had I ever used such a light word to express anything so dark as yearning? "Well, I'm an odd man, Mrs. Watson."

"You're a good man."

I wasn't going to get into that good/bad business with her.

For a time we drank our tea in silence.

"Are you all right, Sherlock?" she asked at last.

I nodded.

She would not be put off. "Try as you might to dismiss this many-worlds business as mere speculation, it bothers you," she observed.

"I can't say 'bother' is the right word."

"What is?"

Entices? Intrigues? Ridicules? There was no single word. "It comes to this," I said. "Life has always seemed to me to be insufficient. Sometimes, unbearably so. Existence as nothing more than a line leading from birth to death, marked along the way by choices that inevitably eliminate far more possibilities than they can ever produce? Insufficient! And yet what else is there but for us to choose? What is that American poem about the road not taken? The poet comes to a fork. 'I took the one less traveled by, and that has made all the difference.' Dash it all, *every* choice makes all the difference. Isn't it such an American characteristic to celebrate the choosing, when the now-unknowable world that awaited the poet on the road 'more traveled by' is lost forever?"

"But there are good choices and bad choices, Sherlock," Mrs. Watson observed.

"Well, there are choices that please us and choices that don't. I'll stipulate to that."

"And the process of choosing is not sufficiently diverting?"

"No," I snapped, more energetically than I'd intended. "I'm sorry Mrs. Watson. But for me it always returns to life lacking depth and breadth, being a mere line, as absent of a third dimension as those original, faked fairies in the little girls' photographs, the ones that are all over the newspaper today."

"But hasn't this past week suggested that a simple, straight line may not be the case?" she surmised.

"Eureka," I said, softly.

She smiled.

"It would please me, soothe me, if one's true existence *were* a solid block of all possibilities, whether or not we perceive it as such," I said. "After all, I have a strong instinct that I am more than just the sum of my choices. As are you, Mrs. Watson. As is everyone. We are, all of us, all possible things. Otherwise . . . a life of near infinite possibility reduced to a mere linear succession of events, why bother?"

She shifted on the bench beside me, turning more to my direction. "But being all possible things must place us sometimes on the side of evil," she observed. "All of us. Even you, Sherlock."

"Oh, I can't begin to guess how often I've inadvertently served evil in this one straight line alone," I observed. "Countless instances. Indeed, did I serve evil by negotiating a position with Mycroft, a murderer as vile as Moriarty? A position that cost a good man his reputation?"

"We've been over the Conan Doyle business, Sherlock. He's alive."

"Yes, but if, in another life, I'd taken a differently principled position and refused to negotiate with my brother, attempting instead to aid Conan Doyle in publishing his alternative Stanley Baldwin article and, in the process, gotten us all killed, would that have made me evil? Or even wrong?"

"No, not evil. Not even wrong. But I, for one, am glad to still be alive, here and now."

"Yes, that mattered to me as well, Mrs. Watson."

"I know. Thank you."

She put her age-spotted hand on my scrawny knee. Nothing forward. Just warm, as friends do. I did not put my hand atop hers, though I knew many in this situation would do so.

Not I. Not in this life.

"In some parallel world, John would still be alive," she observed. "Still with us."

"Yes, some other world."

"Sherlock, mightn't you simply trust Dirac's theory?" She didn't wait for an answer. "Dirac was as you are . . . a genius. True? And, since one can't *dis*prove his assertion, mightn't you simply accept it? All possibilities and identities enacted, each as 'real' as any other. Each as real as this."

Of course that was the appeal of the thing.

But I shook my head. "I can't choose to believe one thing or another. It's not who I am."

She removed her hand from my knee. "Didn't you famously say

that when one has eliminated the impossible, whatever remains, *however improbable*, must be the truth?"

"I may have said it, or, quite honestly, John may have conceived it and merely reported I said it."

"Well, either way you're Sherlock Holmes. Your intellect is unbounded."

"Oh, I'm quite bound up."

She ignored my dismissal. "You're internationally famous, accomplished, respected."

"Yes, I enjoy all those public characterizations, but . . ."

"But what?"

I'd only come here to say goodbye. Besides, I felt emptied of words. So I shook my head, feeling finished. "No more, please."

She set down her tea.

We sat for a long time together in silence.

That was the last time I saw Mrs. Watson.

My negotiations with Mycroft at the Diogenes Club had addressed not only the fate of Conan Doyle, who, until that morning, had posed the most immediate threat to the government's commitment to the *status quo*, but also of Mrs. Watson and myself. While neither she nor I was as inclined as Sir Arthur to race to the newspapers with a good story, we two nonetheless could not be ruled out as potential hazards, according to Mycroft. After all, we'd witnessed the ends to which the government had gone to quash news of the strange manifestation at the home of Lady Vale Owen. Of course, Mrs. Watson and I had no proof of a connection between the shooting of Conan Doyle and that of the blond assassin, no proof of the government's involvement in the overnight re-staffing of the Society for Psychic Research, no proof of a pursuit through the sewers of London, no proof of a conspiracy to murder Dirac and Sir Richard. Still, as Mycroft said, the government did not take chances with potentially dangerous ideas. Or dangerous citizens.

But he and I were brothers, after all.

And I had served the Crown well on numerous occasions, despite myself.

So he offered me exile in precisely the kind of comfortable country residence that most of the world already thought I occupied, be it in the Lake District, the Scottish Highlands, or the Sussex Downs, with the proviso that I never return to London, Cambridge, or Oxford, never entertain visitors, particularly Mrs. Watson, never communicate via telephone, telegraph, or letter, and never write or speak of the events that fill these pages. In return for my isolation, I would be left in peace and, of far greater importance to me, the same would be true for Mrs. Watson, who would be allowed to remain in the Belgravia home she had shared with John. I was prohibited from telling her any such a deal had been struck. But I'd not have told her anyway. Her peace of mind was as important to me as her physical safety.

❧

I call this final chronicle *Uncertainty*, not only in reference to Heisenberg's new theory, but also as a description of the manuscript's own fate. Later today, these pages will be smuggled out of England. In time, they will be hidden in the stacks of a library some place far from here. It likely will be many years before they are found. By then, the name Sherlock Holmes may mean nothing. This is as I have planned since I began writing. But if the name is familiar to you who has discovered this manuscript and read to its conclusion, then I beg that before sharing it with any newspaper or publisher you confirm that Mrs. Watson of Belgravia, London, has passed on and is thereby out of all danger. Though I will not see her again in what is left of my days, numbered in single digits now that I have completed this manuscript, she is dear to me, being the nearest thing I have to family or friend.

EPILOGUE

Buenos Aires, Argentina, 1943

It is three minutes past two o'clock in the morning.

The streets outside are silent but for the occasional caterwauling of the strays that dominate Palermo in the small hours. The private investigator sets the last page of the manuscript facedown atop the others to complete a neat pile on the open space of his cluttered desktop. He takes a deep, steadying breath. He is not tired. Rather, he feels almost overstimulated, due less to the *maté* he has been drinking these hours and more to the enticing possibilities of the handwritten document that has been delivered so innocently into his keeping.

The librarian slumps in the wooden chair opposite, sleeping.

"Señor Borges," the PI says, in a voice neither soft nor loud.

The librarian's eyes open. He sits up straighter in the chair and runs one hand through his thinning hair. "What time is it?" Borges asks, seemingly unaware that he wears a watch.

The PI tells him.

"So you've read the entire thing?" Borges inquires.

The PI nods, tapping the backside of the manuscript's last page with the tip of his ring finger. "You say you've had the handwriting analyzed, Señor Borges? It is truly the work of Holmes?"

Borges nods. "It's authentic."

The PI sits back in his chair.

"I've researched the paper it's written on as well," Borges adds. "The watermark is that of a British company that went out of business in 1930."

"Fingerprints?"

Borges leans forward, fully awakened now by his ardor to explain. "By the use of a somewhat labyrinthine social network, telephoning at great expense one acquaintance who led me to another, who led me to yet another, and so on, I eventually contacted a reliable source at Scotland Yard and learned that Señor Holmes was never fingerprinted."

"Convenient," the PI mutters.

"Your cynicism does not suit you," Borges says. "It is not in your character."

The PI decides to ignore Borges's comment about what may or may not constitute his character. "In truth, it's not the logistics that give me pause, Señor Borges. It's that I have a few doubts, from my own past reading of the famous cases, that Holmes was the sort to derive such personal significance from esoteric concepts. To be troubled by them. Rather, he always seemed to me more likely to just debunk them."

"You refer to the *univers parallèles*?"

The PI nods.

"I believe you've misread the historical Holmes." Borges removes a folded sheet of typing paper from his inside jacket pocket. He unfolds it. Next, he takes from his shirt pocket a pair of thick glasses, which he puts on. "I've reread the accounts," he explains. "Allow me to quote directly from Dr. Watson. In *A Study in Scarlet*, Holmes says, 'One's ideas must be as broad as Nature if they are to interpret Nature' and in 'The Adventure of the Final Problem' he states that 'Of late, I have been tempted to look into the problems furnished by nature rather than those more superficial ones for which our artificial state of society is responsible.' In *The Sign of Four* he virtually anticipates the practical application of quantum mechanics, though the discipline was still decades away from development, when he says, 'while the individual man is an insoluble puzzle, in the aggregate he becomes a mathematical certainty. You can, for example, never foretell what any one man will do, but you can say with precision what an average number will be up to. Individuals vary, but percentages remain constant.' This is how it works for elementary particles, no? And in much the same vein, he is quoted in *The Hound of the Baskervilles* as follows, 'We balance probabilities and choose the most likely. It is the scientific use of the imagination . . .' Do you still think he is merely an exponent of materialism? Well, in *The Valley of Fear*, he describes his method as being far from purely observational. I quote: 'Let me indicate a possible line of thought. It is, I admit, mere imagination; but *how often is imagination the mother of truth?*'"

The PI holds up his palm. "That's enough Borges."

"His words, not mine." The librarian removes his glasses, returning them to his shirt pocket, and refolds the paper, placing it again in his jacket.

"It is my job to be a cynic," the PI says. "That's what you've paid me for."

Borges shrugs in acknowledgment.

"Having said that," the PI continues, "I admit that I am convinced of the manuscript's authenticity. So let us turn to the reason you brought it to me. This man who stalks you, who you say shot at you . . ."

"The blond man."

The PI leans forward, resting his forearms on his desk. "Who have you told about this manuscript?"

"No one."

"Not even your wife?"

"I am not married."

The PI nods. "You said before that you do not think this blond man is after the manuscript merely because of its great value to publishers or collectors of rare books and authentic crime artefacts."

"Correct," Borges answers. "I believe my assault and the continuing threat has to do with the potentially revolutionary aspects of the *univers parallèles* at the core of Holmes's manuscript. I believe there remain powerful interests who oppose the notion. In Holmes's experience, that force was the State. But here, it could still be the Church. Or the State. Or both."

"Fine, Señor Borges, but why is this blond man stalking you rather than simply making you a generous offer to purchase the manuscript or, failing that, stealing it from you?"

"Because, for me, there's more than just the manuscript."

The PI waits, saying nothing.

Borges seems to compose his words in his head before speaking them. "You see, in my dream of you, I experienced something akin to what Conan Doyle experienced in his séance."

"A parallel . . . me?" the PI inquires.

"Yes. In my dream, the details of your entire life, including the secret murder case that has occupied your attentions here these past weeks, were known to me. This is because in the dream you were a character *I had created* for that very crime story. That's right. You, the victim, and the murderer were fictions. And yet, here you are."

"And where is this story?"

Borges shakes his head. "In this world, there is no such story. In this world, you and your murder investigation are as real as I am. But in another world . . ."

The PI grunts his disapproval.

Borges stands and begins pacing the small office as he speaks. "Naturally, I related my strange dream to my friends at the Café Tortoni, where I take my coffee. I trusted them. But perhaps one of them was a spy for the same brand of authorities who objected to Conan Doyle's experience more than a decade ago. Perhaps one of them is an Argentinian Mycroft Holmes. In any case, I am now marked. And it should be no surprise. After all, Poe merely suggested the possibility of alternate worlds and lost his life for doing so. Conan Doyle merely attempted to propose that a living, prospering figure in his world had been observed through inexplicable means to be crippled in another, 'parallel world.' And what happens? Conan Doyle's reputation must be destroyed to spare him assassination. And my dream goes farther. It suggests the unthinkable." He stops.

"Which is?" the PI presses after a moment.

Borges looks him in the eye. "It is that fictional characters in one world might be as real as their author in another. In short, you and me. It is a natural outgrowth of the premise. Infinite worlds, infinite possibilities. However, you must see that for either the Church or the State, such an idea is blasphemy, punishable by death. It is chaos and seeming disorder itself. Hence, the gunshot in the park and, now, the shadowy figure outside my house."

"I am no mere fiction," the PI objects, standing from behind the desk. "I am not your 'creation.' I am flesh and blood."

"In this world that is so."

The PI laughs. "You are not my 'author,' Señor Borges."

"That is true, here and now. But in a multiplicity of universes, I *have* written you into existence, and you have done the same for me," Borges continues. "In some, we've been written into existence by someone else altogether, and in others we are no one's literary creation but are simply real, as we *seem* to be here and now."

The PI is silent.

"As one whose imagination allows for the use of forbidden, ancient languages and geometry to predict the location of a murderer, you must be open to such wonders," Borges implores.

The PI is taken aback. How does the librarian know the details of his other, current case? "It's true that I have a map and a compass from which I have been making calculations regarding the murder of a rabbi and others. And it's also true that I've told no one about these actions, so you demonstrate knowledge whose source is at once disturbing and fascinating. But that is a different case, my dear Señor Borges."

Borges shakes his head. "It is all one."

"I refuse to be distracted from the matter at hand by your aggravating, if accurate, speculations about my work, Señor Borges," the PI expostulates. "Is my method for investigating the rabbi's murder complex? Yes. However, in considering *your* dilemma, which is what you've paid me to do, I believe complexity may be a misstep. For you, the simplest explanation is likely best. Thus, I reassert that, for all the metaphysical fireworks you have attempted to launch here in my office, whoever is shadowing you simply wants to obtain this priceless manuscript, handwritten by the most famous consulting detective ever to live. It is a treasure. All else is simply your overactive imagination."

Borges shakes his head. "Occam's razor does not always slice straight. The universe is a labyrinth."

The PI returns to his swiveling desk chair and sits. He takes a deep, cleansing breath and, with a gesture of his hand, indicates for Borges to return to the wooden chair across the desk to take a seat too.

Borges obliges.

"I base my assertions on my own sensibilities, Señor Borges. You see, *I* would be willing to kill simply to obtain the manuscript, disregarding its philosophical implications altogether. It's worth a fortune. So why wouldn't some other actor be willing to do the same?"

Borges holds up his index finger, like a schoolteacher correcting a well-intentioned but wrongheaded student. "What you say about yourself is not so. Of this I am quite certain because I know your character, having created it elsewhere. You are, above all things, honest."

"But what of the variations that distinguish one universe from another?" the PI presses.

Borges considers, but has no answer.

"Perhaps I am only *almost* the same as the character you wrote, Señor Borges, granting that your dream truly was a window into another existence. Doesn't the word 'alternate' suggest variation, either large or small? So, working from your imaginative premise, I may be nearly the same as your fictional creation, but not quite. Indeed, perhaps I am different at the core of my heart, which happens to be the place that matters most." The PI slides open his desk drawer.

Borges holds up his palm. "I appreciate the opportunity to drink to our honest debate, but I cannot handle more fernet at this hour."

It is not a bottle of fernet that the PI withdraws from the drawer.

This time, it is a handgun.

"You see, Señor Borges, I *am* willing to kill to obtain the manuscript." He aims the weapon.

Borges's eyes fix on the gun.

"I am not a collector of such artifacts myself, but I know some who are," the PI continues. "And they will pay handsomely."

After a moment Borges manages words: "But you can't just shoot me. Someone will hear."

The PI shrugs. "It's after two o'clock in the morning. And this is Palermo. One gunshot? Nothing. Besides, I have friends on the police force. And higher up. And they will believe any story I tell them. What a world, no? Perhaps you'd prefer an alternate one. But I'm afraid this is what you get, here and now."

Borges raises his palms to shoulder level. "Wait, you're my creation. Don't you understand? What are you without me?"

"Wealthy," the PI answers as he pulls the trigger.

The shot rings in the night.

The PI sits for a moment, listening for the return of silence. When it comes, it remains unbroken. He glances at the dead man in the chair across from him before replacing the handgun in his drawer. He will make a phone call to get help disposing of the body. But first he picks up the manuscript, his bounty. It is so light in his hands. He pushes back from the desk and stands, walking past the slumped librarian to the window to confirm that the sound of the gunshot has drawn no attention.

There is no traffic on the street. All is deserted.

He glances across to the Jardines de Palermo, which, likewise, is still. The trees cast shadows. Is that a movement in the park? A tall blond man steps out from behind a jacaranda, his gaze directed up toward the PI's window.

ABOUT THE AUTHOR

Gordon McAlpine is the author of the Edgar® Award–nominated *Woman with a Blue Pencil*, which Joyce Carol Oates described as "a brilliantly structured labyrinth of a novel . . . one that Kafka, Borges, and Nabokov, as well as Dashiell Hammett, would have appreciated." He is also the author of the critically acclaimed novels *Hammett Unwritten*, *Mystery Box*, *The Persistence of Memory*, and *Joy in Mudville*, as well as the award-winning trilogy for middle grade readers, The Misadventures of Edgar and Allan Poe. He lives with his wife, Julie, in Southern California.